Ge1

By

Kitty French

Dear Becky,

Fab to see you again!

love

Kitty xx.

Chapter One

Abel Kingdom wasn't a man accustomed to paying women to take their clothes off.

Even the ready supply of ice cold, free champagne did little to temper his mood as he sat alone in the VIP box at Theatre Divine somewhere in the rainy, Saturday night backstreets of East London. Below him, the hustle of excited patrons sent up a low buzz from the stalls, and the occasional glance that flicked up towards him revealed eyes laced with the expectation of a salacious thrill. Sharply dressed men with territorial arms around the shoulders of their corset-clad wives and girlfriends, there to be titillated, a prelude to their own private shows when they left for their homes and bedrooms later that evening.

Abel didn't share their expectation, nor their heady excitement. The prospect of watching the show did nothing for him and the faded beauty of the old theatre did little more. The peacock-blue velvet seats and tasselled curtains were running towards threadbare and the dulled lustre of the gilt cherubs haloed around the balconies and ceiling embellishments had seen better days. Glossy photographs out in the foyer told stories of star turns and celebrity visitors over the years, but none in recent times. It was a tired, jaded place, yet Abel knew enough to see that beneath its shabby overcoat the bones of the building were still strong and begging for better vestments. And he'd give it better, just as soon as he got through this god-awful evening and sat down to talk numbers with Davey Divine, Theatre Divine's current owner-incumbent.

For the sake of this building, he'd accept the older man's unwanted hospitality. He'd drink his economy champagne, and he'd watch his low-rent show, and then he'd hussle the theatre right out of Davey Divine's hands.

Genie Divine wasn't stupid. Headstrong maybe, and often rash, but she wasn't stupid. Something was up with her Uncle Davey.

He was avoiding her questions, and it hadn't escaped her notice that he'd started to swoop on the mail to prevent her from getting to it first. And if she'd needed any further confirmation of her suspicions, he'd done something that afternoon that he'd never done in all of their years together. He'd locked the office door, a clear 'keep out' message even though he hadn't actually said the words out loud. Scenarios scuttled like beetles through Genie's mind, each more worrying than the last. Was he in trouble? Or, oh God, was he ill?

She placed the liquid eyeliner down on the dressing table, her hand suddenly too shaky to apply a clean line. She'd ask him after they closed up tonight. Taking several deep, calming breaths, Genie unscrewed the lid of an enormous pot of body glitter, lost in thought. Whatever was going on, she was determined to get to the bottom of it before her head hit the pillow tonight. For now though, she needed to put it to the back of her mind. She was due out on stage in under an hour, and as always, the show must go on.

Abel watched Davey Divine run through his outrageous drag act, noting with grudging appreciation that the guy had had the eager crowd eating out of his hand from the moment he'd strutted out into the spotlight. He could practically feel the heat-haze rising from the audience as Divine expertly warmed them up for the main attraction of the night.

The main attraction. Abel ran an irritated finger inside his shirt collar and popped the top button open. Glancing down, his eyes scanned over the flyer on the table beside him, trumpeting tonight's star turn in jaunty, red circus script.

Genie.

One of the capital's best kept secrets!

The sexiest burlesque star in London!

Yeah, right. Weren't they all? Burlesque. Strippers. They were all the same to him. Women who took their clothes off for money. Women who used their bodies to manipulate men. Women who set off alarms in his head for all the wrong reasons. He hadn't set foot inside a strip joint since he'd turned sixteen years old and been old enough to make his own decisions. He glanced at his watch then scrubbed his hand over his chin; bored, aggravated, and mentally calculating how long it would be before this charade was over with and he could get some sense out of Davey Divine.

He was yanked back into the moment by the sultry slide of a trumpet solo from the orchestra pit to herald the shift of mood from bawdy to burlesque. The crowd erupted into spontaneous applause as the house lights dimmed, a lone spotlight drawing every eye to the centre of the stage as the floorboards opened to allow a dazzling golden genie's lamp to rise slowly out from beneath. Encrusted with theatrical jewels, it bounced trippy, rainbow kaleidoscope patterns of light around the auditorium walls. The sexy, evocative musical score conjured Turkish bazaars and snake charmers, and what *was* that scent? Incense? Musk? Spice? Abel leaned forward a little in his seat. He wasn't fooled for a moment by the multiple assaults on his senses, but once more he found himself reluctantly impressed by the level of expertise. These people sure knew how to entertain.

The orchestra swelled the anticipation to a crescendo with a dramatic flourish and the audience reacted accordingly, their applause thunderous when, at last, the hinged lid of the huge lamp opened.

A gasp. A collective intake of breath. And then several

seconds of awe-struck silence as, inch by glorious, creamy inch, the star of the show rose slowly from inside the lamp.

Statuesque and majestic with her back turned towards the audience, she stood with one gloved hand planted on her hip, the other flourishing a huge, ivory ostrich feather fan high above her head.

Despite his best intentions, Abel wasn't bored any more. He reached for his glass without taking his eyes from the stage. He hadn't even seen Genie's face, and already he'd stopped thinking about his business meeting. His eyes followed the nude pink silk corset laced down the length of her delicate back, and the tip of his tongue snaked over his lips as his fingers itched to pull those ribbons open.

The champagne suddenly tasted honey-sweet as it cooled his parched throat. *Jesus*. He hadn't seen curves like that in his life, and he'd seen a lot of curves.

His gaze strayed lower, over the frilled silk knickers that encased the rounded perfection of her ass. He was glad of the solitude of the private box, because he was hard for her already.

Down there on the stage, Genie swept the fan behind her with a wiggle, then dropped the feathers gracefully down back inside the lamp.

Turn around.

She was peeling off those long gloves now and flicking them away from herself carelessly. Her arms as she revealed them were fine boned and feminine. Who knew a bare wrist could be such a turn-on? Abel felt as if he'd been caught watching Victorian pornography. Even though the rational part of his brain warned him that he was falling into her age-old honey trap, the turned-on side of his brain slammed the door on common sense.

Turn around.

Genie ran her hands playfully down the sides of her corset, almost turning to glance out over her shoulder before seeming to change her mind. Frustration spiked through Abel's body as he leaned both elbows on the edge of the box.

Turn around.

Her fingers ran down the length of her legs, all the way to remove her silver spike-heeled stilettos, which followed the fan into the depths of the lamp. She was left bouncing on her stockinged tiptoes to the sliding trumpet fanfare, swaying that delicious ass in a way that had Abel shifting uncomfortably in his seat.

Turn around.

When she flicked open the catches on her stockings and rolled them down her legs like a wartime sweetheart, he emptied the rest of the champagne into his glass, took a hefty slug, and wiped the back of his hand across his lips.

What was this place? A theatre, or a fucking opium den? He was losing his head, and he couldn't seem to rein himself back in. He didn't do this. He didn't lose control. Ever.

'Turn around. For fuck's sake, turn around.' Abel didn't even realise that this time he'd whispered it out loud.

And, as if heeding his words, at long last Genie turned around.

From famine to feast, and he didn't know where to look first. His body burned to see hers, yet it was her face that he found himself most desperate to lay eyes on. Half of him hoped it would break the spell. He knew she'd be attractive. No woman could exude this kind of confidence without the innate knowledge that she was beautiful. But whose kind of beautiful was she? Every woman had her own something special. What was hers? And then he let himself study her, and he knew.

Genie wasn't a pretty girl. She wasn't the kind of girl who'd be chosen for the cheerleading squad. There was nothing cute or girl-next-doorish about her. This girl was pure Hollywood gold, with the kind of face that demanded her angled cheekbones be studio-lit, her Bardot lashes batted flirtatiously, and her lips permanently painted red to match the glossy, pin curled waves of her hair. She looked like a girl who smoked cigarettes and bathed in champagne, who knew every dirty word in the

5

dictionary and a few more besides. He couldn't quite make out the colour of her eyes from his vantage point, but when she turned them momentarily up towards him it seemed that she stripped away a layer of his skin.

And then she glanced carelessly away again, palming her hands over her breasts down to the central clips of her corset. *Flick, flick, flick* - it was open in her hands, and she was tipping her head to one side as if to ask the audience whether she ought to remove it. Clearly the response was an overwhelming yes, and a small smile played over her cupid's bow lips as she shrugged one pretty shoulder and then flung the corset wide.

This wasn't Victorian smut any longer, and boy, she was well past the point of a wartime sweetheart. Genie was a harlot, and her body - clad now only in silk knickers and rhinestone encrusted nipple covers - was a sight that had Abel all but ready to vault from the balcony and screw her hard against the side of that fuck-off lamp. *Christ.* She almost laughed with delight as she twirled the corset high in the air and then dropped it into the lamp, taking a moment to flip the lid shut with her toe.

Her ethereally pale skin glittered as if someone had dipped her in stardust, and the high, round fullness of her breasts made him physically ache. Yet another reason she could never be considered a girl next door. If girls next door looked like this, the world would grind to a halt because no one would ever leave home.

He wanted to touch her, to fuck her, to possess her every which way. To lay her on velvet and take her slowly until she moaned his name. To rut her naked up against a rough alley wall until the skin on her shoulder blades bled. In fact, what he really wanted at that moment was to march on stage and throw his jacket around her shoulders to stop every other man in the room from wanting the same thing. But then... no, he didn't want to stop her, because she'd just hitched her thumbs suggestively down the sides of those frilly silk knickers.

She wasn't going to take them off, was she? Abel had his answer in seconds as she shimmied them down her thighs to reveal a tiny, jewelled g-string that did more to frustrate than to satisfy. The girl was practically naked, and still it wasn't enough. He watched her, hypnotised, as she lay down and writhed with pure abandon across the top of the lamp, tracking the rise and fall of her body with his eyes, the feline arch of her spine as she threw her head back and let the endless red waves of her hair tumble behind her.

Every breath in the house sucked in when she lifted an amused, knowing eyebrow towards the audience and reached for those sequinned nipple caps. *Would she bare her breasts?* Just as it seemed to Abel that yes, actually she would, she smiled wickedly and the spotlight blinked out. The show was over.

He dropped his head into his hands in the darkness. She'd looked for all the world like a woman being made love to on top of that lamp, like a woman in the throes of the best orgasm of her life.

No way.

If there was one clear and certain thought in Abel Kingdom's head, it was that he was going to be the one responsible for giving that girl the best orgasm of her life.

But as the house lights came up and common sense seeped back in to his mind, Abel realised with a sudden wash of loathing that he'd been well and truly played. Genie was the consummate showgirl; she knew just how to make the most of what Mother Nature had given her. Self-disgust twisted his gut at the way she'd forced such a visceral, animal reaction out of him. He knew her sort of woman of old, knew that she would be all smoke and mirrors. Yet still he'd found himself unable to take his damn eyes off her, and he hated himself for it almost as much as he hated her now that she was no longer weaving her black magic on the stage.

Was this why Divine had insisted he watch the show before their meeting? Did he think him such a malleable fool that he'd be weakened by the tawdry curves of a temptress and a few glasses of cheap champagne? The worst of it was that he hadn't been far from the mark, for a few moments at least. Abel shoved himself roughly out of the chair and headed for the exit stairs. Divine could wait until morning. Right now he needed to get out of this goddamn place, to let the cool rain wash the sour stench of unwelcome memories from his skin.

Chapter Two

Genie glanced towards her dressing room door in the mirror as someone rapped on it and then pushed it open without waiting for her to shout 'come in.' Deanna's slender frame sidled around the door, her camera slung over her kitsch Barbie and Ken T-shirt and a mug of tea in her hand.

'Tea for the superstar.' She grinned and placed the mug down on Genie's dressing table then parked her skinny backside on the radiator alongside it.

'Cheers, doll.' Genie winced as she peeled off her welded on false eyelashes. 'So, how did it look?'

Her best friend clapped with delight. 'Holy fuck, it looked amazing, G! Better than we even thought it would.' A worried frown crossed Deanna's face. 'Did it feel secure?'

Genie nodded. 'Safe as houses. You're officially a genius.'

Deanna had spent the best part of the last three months painstakingly designing and building the elaborate lamp set, and tonight had been its maiden outing. 'Our best yet, deffo. I took a load of footage for you to see it for yourself.' Her heavy black fringe, patterned this week with electric blue stripes, fell into her eyes as she leaned forward and slid an SD card out of the camera onto the table.

'So, who was the stud-muffin up in the VIP box tonight?' she asked. 'Davey had the staff falling over themselves to ply him with free champagne before the show.'

Genie caught her friend's eye in the mirror, non-plussed. She hadn't noticed any of tonight's audience individually, but then she seldom did when she was out there on the stage. The more unsettling question was why her uncle was giving away free champagne, given his recent tightening of the purse strings. She mentally filed the question away alongside the others she was saving for when she cornered him later.

'I've no clue. I didn't see him.'

'Well, he certainly saw you. I'd like to think it was the lamp that had him enthralled, but from the way he looked at you there was only one thing on his mind.' Deanna whistled. 'And he was hot. Like, super-hot. Like I-want-to-lick-your-face-but-I'm-scared-I'd-burn-my-tongue hot.' She licked her index finger and made a sizzling sound.

Genie laughed. 'Well, I'm sorry I missed him now.' And she was. Attractive men were in woefully thin supply in her life lately, especially ones hot enough to singe body parts, fingers or otherwise.

'C'est la vie, girlfriend.' Deanna slid off the radiator and dropped a quick kiss on Genie's cheek. 'I'm outta here. I'm starving.'

She rubbed a hand over her ironing board stomach and skipped towards the door, turning back as she opened it. 'You really did look great out there tonight, G,' she said softly, every bit the supportive sister that she was as good as. 'Proud of you.'

Genie nodded. 'Proud of you too. We make a good team.'

She looked at the door for a few seconds after Deanna had closed it, unexpected tears welling in her eyes as she cradled her mug in her hands. Life hadn't blessed her with a big, close family, but she'd certainly been blessed with Davey and Deanna, or the double Ds, as she'd affectionately dubbed them. Between them they were her mother, her father, her sister, her brother, and her best friends. She barely ever spared a thought for her birth mother any more, aside from thanking her lucky stars that the woman had at least had the foresight to abandon her baby girl on the steps of her brother's theatre rather than handing her over to some municipal institution.

Half an hour later, and Genie's search for her uncle proved fruitless. His office door was locked once again and his apartment silent and empty. He'd split the top floor of the theatre into two apartments some years back to give them both individual living spaces. He'd said at the time that it was to give her her own bath to hang her smalls over, but Genie knew in her heart that Davey had gone to the trouble in order to keep her close.

Together they'd lived and breathed Theatre Divine for the last twenty-eight years – Genie's whole life. It was their home, their shelter and their first love. Or it always had been, until Davey had fallen head over heels for the fabulously normal and very Californian Robin Delaney. These days Davey and Robin were inseparable and insufferably happy, aside from the fact that Robin missed his sunshine-drenched home on the West Coast and made no secret of the fact that he hoped they'd retire out there soon. Fond as she was of Robin, Genie couldn't contemplate the idea of losing her uncle to the other side of the world.

Having checked every possible place he might be without success, she resigned herself to talking to him first thing in the morning and made her way back upstairs.

Upstairs in the loft a few minutes later, Genie locked her door and flung herself down onto the overstuffed sofa, glad of both the solitude and the comfort. She was tired, but still way too wired after the performance to sleep. Reaching for her bag, she slipped Deanna's SD card into her laptop and slumped back against the welcoming cushions to review the footage of the lamp's first appearance. The auditorium swam into focus on the screen, obviously still early in the evening as the lights hadn't yet gone down and people were milling around in front of the lens to find their seats. Genie's impatient fingers hovered ready to fast-forward, then stilled as the camera panned up to the box, to the man sitting alone with his champagne glass balanced on the edge of the box.

Stud-muffin. Wasn't that what Deanna had said? She'd got that much right at least.

Genie wasn't surprised to see the camera linger on him for longer than was necessary. The guy was making love to the camera lens without even knowing it was there.

Brooding? Oh yes.

Gorgeous? Big green tick.

Stud-muffin? The phrase could have been invented especially for him.

But beautiful as he undoubtedly was, it was his expression that had Genie leaning forward in her seat to study him more closely.

Bleak. Bitter. And very, very complicated.

The guarded expression in his dark eyes hinted at a million things that made her heart lurch unexpectedly, made her want to physically reach out and soothe that scowl from his brow with her fingertips as he pushed his hands through his hair and sighed heavily.

A sharp pang of disappointment prodded Genie in the ribs as the camera tracked away from him to settle on the stage as the curtains went back.

Deanna had also been right on the money about the lamp, though. It looked fabulous centre stage, but Genie was too distracted to give it all the attention it deserved. Keen as she was to review the performance, what she really wanted was for the camera to go back and pick out the enigmatic stranger in the audience.

She didn't have to wait for long. Deanna obviously hadn't been able to resist the urge to pan around the audience part way through the show and rest once again on the VIP box. Genie couldn't really blame her. She may have been flouncing around in nipple tassels on the stage, but Mr Stud-muffin was by far the most fascinating subject in the room.

Except when the camera found him second time around, his expression had shifted from complicated to easy as ABC to read.

He certainly *wasn't* bored any more.

Or bleak.

A soft gasp escaped Genie's lips as she watched him, watching her.

Raw hunger had replaced the bitterness in his eyes.

Hot, naked desire was written all over his face.

He reached out for his champagne without taking his eyes from the stage, then knocked it back in one fluid movement and wiped the back of his hand across the full, sensuous curve of his mouth. *Jesus.* Her blood quickened in her veins and her breath caught in her chest as Deanna tracked in closer on his face. Genie drew her bottom lip into her mouth and bit down slowly as he caught his knuckle between his teeth and held it there as he studied her. He was turned on, and – belatedly and quite unknowingly - he was turning her on too.

'No!' The moan of frustration slipped from her lips as the camera moved back to the on-stage action.

Go back!

Genie could barely watch as she willed Deanna to skim the lens back to the box. As the performance ended and the curtains swept shut, Deanna finally did so. And there was the box again, this time quite empty. He was gone. *Fuck.*

Genie shook her head, clearing her thoughts. Disappointment warred with confusion and frustration in her gut. What just happened there? How the hell had she ended up feeling like the voyeur when he was the one watching her take her clothes off?

Chapter Three

Just after ten the following morning, and Genie wasn't taking no for an answer. She barrelled into her uncle's office without pausing to knock, ready to demand answers to the difficult questions that had filled her sleepless night. She hated feeling so on edge, braced for bad news that seemed to be lurking just around the corner. Whatever was going on, it was better to know what she was up against. What her uncle was up against. What *they* were up against.

Davey looked up, startled as she flew into the room.

'Uncle Davey, listen…' Genie burst out, and then stopped again just as abruptly.

Her uncle wasn't alone. There was a second man in the room, someone with his back turned towards the door as he lounged in the chair at the desk.

'I'm sorry, I didn't realise you had company…' her words tailed off, but she didn't miss the dull flush that crept up her uncle's neck as he looked at her, nor could he hide the strained look in his eyes. What was that? Guilt? Pity? Whatever it was, she didn't like it one bit.

'Now's not a good time, G,' he murmured, and his eyes darted from her face to the man opposite him, and then just as quickly back to her face again, as if there was a chance that she might not notice the guy if he didn't draw her attention to him.

Not a chance in hell. Even with his back towards her, this wasn't the kind of man she, or anyone else, could miss. Broad shouldered and dark haired, he filled his chair and then some, and there was a heady scent in the room that wasn't usually there. Genie stalled on the spot, uncharacteristically knocked off her stride by the stranger's presence. As she deliberated whether to stay or go, he twisted around in his chair to see who had interrupted his meeting.

It was him. *Mr VIP Stud-muffin*. And shit, if he wasn't even better in the daylight than in the night shadows of Deanna's video. He had an undeniable presence, the kind of commanding aura that drew eyes and made people listen, the kind of instant charisma that performers would love to bottle and couldn't fake no matter how hard they worked at it.

His eyes settled on Genie, and she watched the frown flicker over his features. She knew why. He was trying to place her. It happened often, people would see her off stage and not instantly recognise her with her clothes on. Not that they could be blamed: Genie's everyday uniform of battered jeans and tee was a world away from the sequinned nipple tassels and thong. Make-up free, she'd scraped her trademark red hair back into a messy bun at the nape of her neck. She was more student than seductress, and at that moment she was glad of her disguise because Mr VIP was staring at her like a wolf assessing his prey, and despite her hair colour, Genie had no desire to play Little Red Riding Hood.

Her uncle cleared his throat, obviously uncomfortable. 'Please, G. Later?'

Genie swallowed hard, instinctively stepping backwards to escape the hunter. *Who the hell was he?*

Whoever he was, his easy, self-assured laugh filled her ears as she pulled the door closed, and his accompanying words irritated the hell out of her.

'This is one hell of a place you've got here, Mr Divine. Even the cleaner's sexy.'

Down on the stage, Genie circled the lamp assessingly, inspecting it for signs of wear and tear after its first live deployment. She didn't really anticipate any issues, because Deanna was as good as they came at her job, but she knew all too well how vital it was that her central prop was in perfect condition for every single performance. Professionalism demanded that she run her hands over the swooping curves and arches of the prop. As her deft fingers examined, her enquiring mind whirred.

What was his accent? She'd heard enough to deduce that stud-muffin wasn't English, but not quite enough to place him accurately. American? Australian? And why the hell was he here for a second day on the run? He'd been closeted up with her uncle for more than an hour now; she knew because she'd have heard him leave in the quiet, closed theatre.

Cleaner. Pfft. A typical, arrogant man making typical, arrogant assumptions. The fact was that Genie very often swept the stage after performances because the glitter got places glitter had no place to be. It was an occupational hazard, but it drove their chief cleaning lady crazy. Wilma had been with them for as long as Genie could remember, as necessary a part of the theatre as Davey or Genie herself. Anyway, what *she* did wasn't the point. What *he* did was the burning question, and on cue, the staff door to the side of the stalls opened and her uncle and the stud-muffin appeared.

Spontaneously, Genie found herself sliding into the shadows behind the lamp. She knew it was wrong to eavesdrop, but then she wasn't a girl who was big on following the rules for the sake of it. Peering meerkat-like over the handle of the lamp, she watched as her uncle extended his hand and smiled.

'It was good to meet you at last, Mr Kingdom.' Davey pumped his guest's hand up and down with a little too much enthusiasm for Genie's liking. And, err, hello? *Mr Kingdom?* No way was that his actual name. She couldn't see Stud-muffin's face because once again he had his back turned to her, but she could hear his voice as clearly as any actor's on the stage, as it echoed around in the theatre's helpful acoustics.

'You too, Mr Divine, you too. I'll be in touch.' *Australian.* Not a strong accent, but an unmistakable hint.

'Soon, I hope?' There was an edge of desperation to her uncle's tone that rang Genie's alarm bells.

'For sure.'

It struck her suddenly that once stud-muffin left the building, she was reliant on her uncle to put her in the picture about what exactly was going on here. Would his inherent instinct to protect her stop him from being completely candid? She couldn't risk it. Genie had long ago learned to trust her gut, and right now it was telling her to get her ass out from behind the lamp and find a way to get her uncle's guest alone. Painting on her game face, she sauntered out of the shadows and feigned surprise at finding company in the room as she skipped down the side steps towards them.

'I thought I heard voices,' she smiled, wiping her palms on her backside.

Both men looked her way, one in clear discomfort and the other with predatory interest.

Her uncle's smile didn't quite make it as far as his eyes. 'I'll be with you in a sec love, let me just see Mr Kingdom out.'

Uh-uh. That wasn't going to work. 'Let me. I'm heading that way anyway.' She smiled brightly to mask the lie. 'I'll come up and find you in five.'

Short of insisting, she'd left her uncle nowhere to go but back through the door he'd just appeared from, and although his frown told her he was ill at ease, he left and clicked it closed behind him. Genie inclined her head for their guest to follow her out through the auditorium, just in case her uncle had paused on the other side of the door to listen. As she reached the reception kiosk, she finally turned to look Stud-muffin in the eyes. Mistake number one. He had killer eyes. Dark, so dark it was hard to make out any colour around the pupil. Intense, and at that moment trained on her so hard they grazed her soul. She wanted to look away and found she couldn't.

What big eyes you have.
All the better to see you with.

'Who are you?'

The simple words were the only ones she could scramble together. If the man said he was Jesus himself, she'd probably believe him. Or the devil incarnate.

He shifted his weight onto his other foot and folded his arms across the broad expanse of his chest as he regarded her in silence. Her uncle had addressed him formally, and yet he wasn't dressed in business attire. His clothes clung to him like a possessive lover: well worn jeans and a navy tee that obviously knew his body intimately.

'It's a pleasure to meet you too, honey,' he said, choosing not to answer her question. There was that hint of arrogance again in the amused set of his jaw as he ran his hand over the dark beginnings of stubble there. Genie's eyes followed the movement. He had good hands. Strong, golden tanned, with short, squared off nails.

What big hands you have.
All the better to touch you with.

'What's your business with David?'

Genie knew that her line of questioning was far too direct, but he had her on the back foot with all this eye-fucking.

He raised one nonchalant shoulder and the curve of a smile played over his lips. *His lips. Fuck.* He had the kind of mouth you want to watch slide over your nipple.

What a big mouth you have.
All the better to eat you with.

Genie wanted to be eaten.

This wasn't going to plan.

'Are you his security guard as well as his cleaner?'

Stud-muffin's sarcasm snapped her out of her fairytale fantasy sharpish. It was becoming clear that he was almost as unlikely to tell her the truth as her uncle was.

'I'm not his cleaner,' she said, wishing her hands hadn't

planted themselves on her hips, Mae West-style. 'I'm his niece, and the assistant manager of this theatre.'

She wasn't, officially, but she was as good as.

'Is that so?' he said. 'Then you really ought to know who I am already.'

Genie's fingernails dug into her palms in agitation. It occurred to her that he ought to know who she was too, given the way he'd looked at her last night. It seemed that they were both in the dark. Drawing in a measured breath, she relaxed her shoulders and changed tack. Maybe she'd get more out of him with honey than vinegar.

Flexing her fingers out, she folded her arms lightly beneath her breasts and tipped her head a little to the side. His eyebrows raised a fraction in response, and to his credit he didn't lower his eyes from her face for even the slightest moment.

'I'm sorry, that was rude of me,' she said, throwing in a rueful smile for good measure. 'Late nights and early mornings don't agree with me.'

His shoulders relaxed a little, mirroring hers, and his dark eyes acknowledged her change of tone with interest. 'You better get back to bed then, baby,' he murmured. 'Want me to come and sing you a lullaby?'

He shrugged when her eyebrows inched up her head. 'Sorry, was that rude of me?' His expression told her he knew damn well it was and he couldn't care less.

'And presumptuous too, given that I don't even know your name,' she shot back, keeping her tone light, even though his overt flirting had rattled her composure.

He held his hand out across the space between them. 'Abel Kingdom.'

Genie licked her lips and reached out her hand towards his.

'If I shake your hand, it doesn't mean you get to sing me to sleep,' she said, and then inhaled sharply when his fingers closed around hers. Heat. Strength. *Erotic.*

'Who said anything about sleeping?' he said, holding on to

both her hand and her gaze for longer than necessary. Did his thumb just stroke over her palm? She couldn't be certain.

'Funny guy, huh?' Genie extracted her hand slowly. 'Abel Kingdom.' She said his name out loud and let it hang in the air between them. 'Is that your real name?'

'Am I to add private detective to your long and wildly varied job description?'

Genie glanced away for a second, unable to gather her thoughts whilst looking at him. 'Just looking out for my own.'

His eyes had turned serious when she looked up again, and he pulled a card from his back pocket. 'It's my real name.' He put the card in her hand. 'Tell me yours.'

She sighed, unsure if she wanted him to connect the dots. The card in her fingers was still warm from being tucked against his ass. Tracing a finger over his name, her eyes skimmed the words. Abel Kingdom. Director. Kingdom Fitness and Wellbeing.

'Fitness?' Genie said, intending it to be a question, and before she could check herself her eyes moved instinctively over his biceps. His clothes did nothing to disguise the fact that he was hot as hell and had a body that would no doubt look even better naked.

When she met his eyes again he nodded.

'As in gyms?'

He nodded for a second time, shrugged one shoulder. 'That kind of thing, yeah.'

Genie's mind ran in circles. What did her uncle want with a gym owner? He certainly wasn't in the market for a personal trainer. She needed to know more.

'Want me to tell you about it over dinner, green eyes?'

He couldn't have asked a more timely question, yet still she stalled. He spoke again when she didn't.

'Do you have a pen?'

She leaned over reception and reached one from the desk, holding it out to him when she turned back around. Instead of taking the pen he offered her his forearm. 'Write your number down. I'll text you about dinner.'

Genie looked at him quizzically. 'You want me to write my number on your arm?'

He nodded innocently.

'You don't have a mobile I can just key it into?'

He shook his head. 'Not one with any life in, anyway.'

'I could write it on a scrap of paper?'

'I might lose it.' He stretched his forearm out a little further and turned it over, wrist side up, his eyes locked on hers. 'I don't want to lose it.'

Genie clicked the pen open and stepped closer to him. She needed to be closer still. It crossed her mind that he could just as easily write it on his own arm, but then she also knew that his phone was probably fully juiced up and chances were he wouldn't have lost a slip of paper either.

He was flirting with her, testing out her boundaries like kids playing chicken to discern who was the leader of the pack. She knew the rules, but she was no chicken herself and she knew how to bend them. Stepping so close that she could feel his body heat, she closed her fingers around his wrist to hold his arm steady. He was warm and vital, and she could feel his steady pulse beating beneath her fingertips.

How could he be iron hard to the touch, yet his skin felt like silk? And why did this whole thing feel so inappropriately intimate? She wasn't even looking at him, but his breath warmed her ear as the nib started to roll gracefully across the golden expanse of his arm. They both watched as the ink marked his skin, a swirled tattoo branding him with her details.

'Is now a good time to tell you it's permanent ink?' she said as she wrote, hyper aware that her hip had brushed his crotch.

'Good,' he breathed. 'Is now a good time to tell you I want to fuck you tonight?'

Genie gasped softly, glad to have finished writing because his words had just shut her brain down. She tilted her head up to look at him, and found him waiting for her with that cocky hint of a half smile on his lips again, but his dark eyes told her he wasn't joking.

'Are you always this forward?' she asked, aware that her fingers were still curved around his wrist. She let her thumb circle slowly over his pulse. He could try to assert lazy authority with his words as much as he liked, but his quickened pulse told Genie all she needed to know. She was in charge here. And then he reached out and brushed the back of his warm fingers fleetingly across her cheekbone, and, easy as that, he was back in the driving seat.

He tucked an errant lock of her hair behind her ear. 'Yes.'

Time seemed suspended, matrix style, as Genie caught her breath and stared at him. He really was outlandishly beautiful. Just like his clothes, his dark hair was the antithesis of business smart, too long and waving over his forehead and collar. The dark shadow of stubble couldn't hide his strong jaw, and her fingers itched to feel it. Was it fresh and spiky, the kind of stubble that left its mark on the tender skin of a woman's inner thighs? Or was it a few days old and as silken as the skin of his forearms?

The slight indentation in his nose spoke of a bar brawl, a theory backed up by the fine hairline scar that tracked across his cheekbone. What had he fought over? A woman, maybe? Was he a man who'd fight to defend his girl's honour? Instinct told her yes. She needed to double check that business card of his to make sure it didn't actually say Clark Kent, because despite the lack of lycra, he was already half-way to smouldering superhero right here in the auditorium.

Kiss me… the single thought filled her head so urgently that she wondered if he could see it running like ticker tape across her eyes.

Put your mouth on my mouth, Abel Kingdom.

Her eyes dropped to his lips, parted just enough to slide her tongue in and taste him. She stepped against him when his hand slid around the back of her neck, drawing her head to his. Her eyelids closed as she offered him her mouth, and a shiver of pleasure rippled down her spine as the warmth of his breath mingled with hers. An even stronger shudder of frustration ran through her body when he turned his head a fraction and let his lips linger against her cheek rather than her mouth.

'Tonight,' he murmured, stroking the back of her neck as he kissed her jaw before turning and leaving through the revolving door without glancing back.

Genie watched him, touching her fingers against her cheek in shock. On the surface, she'd accepted his dinner invitation to find out more about his business with her uncle. But scratch that surface and another reason was now written as clearly as her number on his arm. She'd said yes because she wanted Abel Kingdom's kiss, and a whole lot more besides.

Abel waited until he was a decent distance from the theatre and pulled his mobile out of his pocket. He keyed the number from his arm into it as he walked, his mind on his meeting with Davey Divine.

Much as the older guy had tried to hide his desperation, it had been abundantly clear that he needed to offload the theatre quickly. Abel wanted it. He wanted it, but not at the price that Davey Divine was asking for it.

Listening to the man speak, it had become obvious that there was only one real fly in the ointment, and as was so often the case, it was sentiment. The theatre had been in the Divine family for generations and Davey loved the place, but more worryingly, he'd spoken of how devastated his beloved niece would be if he sold up. It was a delicate situation that demanded careful negotiation, and as Abel's mind had scrabbled for the right tack the door had flown open and the girl in question had slammed into the office like a small hurricane. This was Divine's niece? This slender, studious looking girl? He'd sized her up, the hint of her curves beneath her clothes, her snatched back hair, her face bare of any trace of make-up. She'd seemed somehow out of place amongst the gloss and glitz of theatre-land, too pure and real for her heart to belong there. Abel's sharp mind had found the tack it needed. If this slip of a girl was all that stood in the way of the deal, then it was as good as signed, sealed and delivered already.

It was only when he'd met her for a second time that he'd seen the glint of steel behind her clear green eyes, and the proud set of determination to her delicate jaw. Good. He didn't enjoy taking candy from babies. He much preferred a challenge, the clash of swords, the blood of battle before victory, because he always, always won.

Had he come on too strong? Probably. Had he planned on it? Hell, no. *Is now a good time to tell you I want to fuck you tonight?* The words should have stayed in his goddamn head, he knew better than to play his hand too early. It made her a much more formidable adversary, knowing that she could affect him like this. Almost deadly. He wanted her body and her theatre, but he feared he needed to have them in the opposite order.

Chapter Four

He still didn't know who she was. It wasn't unusual: her stage persona required so much make-up and embellishment that few people made the real life connection instantly. Genie sensed that Abel Kingdom hadn't slotted the pieces together, and she was perfectly happy for it to stay that way, at least until she found out the precise nature of his business with her uncle.

She'd tried unsuccessfully to winkle information from Davey earlier in the afternoon, but he'd clammed up tighter than an oyster being ransacked for its pearl. She'd made the spot decision not to tell him about her dinner meeting with Abel Kingdom, even though keeping secrets from him left her feeling shoddy and underhand. She wasn't accustomed to there being anything but easy honesty between herself and her uncle, and she could only pray that she was doing the right thing. She uneasily squared it with herself by thinking of it as protecting him, although God knew what from. Abel Kingdom didn't seem like a loan shark trying to extract debt by force, but there was an undeniably ruthless edge to him that had her watchful all the same.

Is now a good time to tell you I want to fuck you tonight?

Any man with the balls to drop that into an opening conversation with a stranger needed watching closely.

And that was another reason to keep an eye on him. He didn't feel like a stranger, even though she knew nothing of him aside from his name and that he felt like silk. He was different from any man she'd ever met before. It wasn't just his physical presence, even though he stood a good head taller than she was. And it wasn't just his beauty, or the edge of arrogance threaded through his words. It was all of that and more. He radiated danger, and for some unfathomable reason Genie found that his sexiest trait of all.

She stilled for a second on the steps of the swish old hotel Abel's text had suggested they meet at, taking a moment to prepare herself. She could do this. *She could do this.* Painting a faux confident smile on her face, she stepped up towards the waiting doorman and passed through the glass doors into the marble vestibule. She was a few minutes early, deliberately so in order to be there before him. If she was going to lay a honey trap, she needed to be in complete control from the moment they met.

Abel sat at the sweeping bar, nursing a scotch between his hands. People milled around him, businessmen and lovers making the most of a quiet Sunday evening before the grind of a new week. Being back in London didn't suit him. He missed the wide skies and open spaces of home, not to mention the warmth of both the sunshine and the people who'd welcomed him as one of their own.

All of his memories of London were bad ones. Would tonight be more pleasurable, perhaps? It was business on one level, but then… it hadn't been business on his mind when he'd thought of her earlier as he'd showered, and again as he'd dressed. He didn't even know her fucking name, yet he was thinking about fucking her and making her forget it.

He watched in the bevelled mirrors behind the bar as a woman came in, pausing in the doorway to sweep her gaze around the room.

His body reacted before his head had time to, alerting him like an early warning system. She looked a world away from the fresh-faced girl he'd propositioned that morning. Gone were the jeans and messy hair, replaced with a midnight blue silk dress that wrapped around her body and knotted on her hip in a way that suggested one good tug on those trailing ties and the whole thing might fall off. It was almost demure, aside from the fact that it highlighted the curve of her waist and the swell of her breasts in a way that told the world that beneath that dress, the woman was pure fucking dynamite.

He found himself breathing in sharply as her gaze finally came to rest on him, and he slid to his feet as she moved across the room. He was a man, which made him aware than every other man in the room had noticed her too with varying degrees of obviousness. This morning she'd looked like a college student. This evening she looked like a highly fuckable business executive. She was a chameleon, and it only served to make her all the more intriguing.

'Abel,' she said, and hearing his name on her lips for the first time made him want to hear her say it again when he was buried balls deep inside her.

'You look incredible,' he murmured, intoxicated by the sweet, clean scent of her as he dipped his head to brush a kiss across her cheek.

She drew back her head a little and looked at him with those incredible clear green eyes. 'I have a mouth. Kiss it.'

Did she actually just fucking say what he thought she said? Shock registered first, then a bolt of lust that shot straight to his cock.

'Christ all-fucking-mighty,' he ground out, pulling her against him, one hand clamped around the nape of her neck, the other sliding over her silk-encased ass. He moulded her to him and lowered his head, noting with satisfaction the momentary flare of apprehension that registered in her eyes a second before his lips touched hers.

Kissing someone for the first time generally involved a degree of anticipation and build up. Not this time. He took her mouth hard and heavy, licking his tongue over hers when she opened up for him. Seriously, the girl had him so hot that if he could have rucked that dress up around her hips and screwed her bent over the nearest bar stool, he would have. A low sexual sound of appreciation drifted from her mouth into his, an involuntary reaction to a kiss that came out of nowhere and melted your bones. It was the French kiss of lovers on Parisian street corners: intense, deep, and open mouthed; drenched in sexual potential. He bit down on the softness of her bottom lip when she wrapped her arms around him, her fingernails raking over the skin at the nape of his neck.

He held her ass hard against him as he spoke to her softly, a lethal whisper, his mouth now pressed to her ear.

'Say something like that to me in public again and it won't be my tongue in your mouth. It'll be my cock.'

Her sharp intake of breath gratified him. She'd deliberately set out to shock him, and to give her her dues, she'd caught him off guard for a few seconds back there.

'I have a mouth. Kiss it.' Fuck, he'd have been proud of that line himself. He was already enjoying the evening even more than he'd hoped.

Genie reeled as Abel set her back down on her feet. Hers had been a line designed to show him that she was no pushover, but his kiss and his comeback had shown her in no uncertain terms that she was playing the game with a master.

Right. Regroup required. She smoothed her hands down her dress and then looked up at him with a sweet smile. 'Is that the usual way to greet your date in Australia?'

'Only dates with a smart mouth.'

Abel's gaze dropped to her lips, and she traced the tip of her tongue slowly across her top lip for his benefit. Or to be more precise, for his downfall.

'You don't like my mouth?'

'I liked kissing it just fine.' He looked at her mouth for a few long seconds, as if he were about to do it again.

Genie nodded. 'That's good, Abel, because if you're really nice to me tonight, I might let you do it again later.' Quite how such brave words were leaving her mouth she had no clue, because inside she felt anything but brave. 'Shall we eat?'

Abel folded his menu and handed it to the waiter after they'd ordered. 'So. What does the G stand for?'

Genie had expected the question to come up.

'G?'

'You still haven't told me your name. Your uncle called you G. What is it? Gina? Gayle?' He shrugged. 'Gert?'

She laughed lightly, affecting nonchalance. 'It's Gigi, but most people just call me G.' It wasn't really a lie. Gigi had been her childhood nickname, even if it wasn't technically her given name.

'Gigi.' Abel said it as if he were testing it, and his face said he wasn't especially impressed. 'Sounds more like a circus horse than a woman to me.'

Genie almost spat her wine back into her glass. 'I'm sorry?'

If he didn't like Gigi, he was going to be even less impressed with Genie.

He shrugged, thoroughly unfazed by her shock. 'No offence.'

She placed her wine glass down on the table. 'Do you think you could at least pretend to be polite?'

'It doesn't mean I like you any less because I don't like your name,' he said. 'I'll just think of something else to call you.'

Genie opened her mouth to answer him and then closed it again as the waiter reappeared with their starters. She was actually quite glad of the interruption, because the idea of him inventing his own private name for her did weird things to her insides.

The food was every bit as glamorous and grand as the hotel, and delicious enough to stall their conversation in order to appreciate it fully. She looked up as Abel reached for the chilled Sauvignon.

'More wine… red?'

She glanced at the white wine in confusion. 'Red?'

'A potential nickname. Assuming you *are* actually a redhead?' He topped up her glass. 'Actually, no. Forget it. It doesn't suit you anyway.'

Ouch. This guy had a lot to learn about charm.

'My hair colour doesn't suit me?'

'Your hair colour suits you just fine,' he said. 'But the nickname doesn't.'

'I'm almost afraid to ask why not,' she muttered. This was becoming less like a conversation and more like a verbal assault course.

Her eyes were drawn to his hands as he picked up his wine glass. Strong, tanned and sure, the impossibly delicate crystal he held looked in dire danger.

'It's too hard. Too factual. Too... newsreader.'

'I could be a newsreader if I wanted to,' she shot back, nettled by his assumption.

'No way,' he laughed lightly. 'You'd be too much of a distraction.'

It was a compliment of sorts, even if not of the usual sort.

Their main courses arrived, stalling conversation for a second time; thick, pink lamb rump for Abel, coral bright salmon in a delicate watercress sauce for Genie.

'Tell me more about what you do, Abel,' Genie said, sipping her wine and glancing at him casually over the rim of her glass. 'Is it just the one gym you have, or a whole chain of them?' She needed to get him talking about his business, steer the conversation around to the nature of his interest in her uncle.

He sliced his lamb through and looked at her across the table.

'I'm not fond of the word chain, but I guess it works. Seventeen and counting.'

Genie's eyes widened. 'Wow. All in Australia?'

'For now... Bunny.'

'I beg your pardon?'

'Bunny. As in Jessica Rabbit.' He placed his knife and fork down as he regarded her across the table. 'Red hair. Ivory skin. And...' his voice trailed off and his eyes flickered briefly down her body. 'Curves.'

'Do I have a say in this?' she said. In truth, she was a little disappointed in him. It seemed a lazy comparison, especially given her occupation, even if he *wasn't* yet aware of it.

'No. But don't worry, it won't be Jessica. I'm looking for something more… personal.'

Glad as she was to hear that 'Jessica' was off the menu, Genie didn't want to spend the evening talking about nicknames. She toyed with the stem of her wine glass.

'Have you always worked for yourself?'

'Pretty much.' He shrugged unapologetically. 'I don't get along well with other people telling me what to do.'

Well, that came as a surprise to no one. 'You didn't seem to mind back in the bar earlier.'

Abel's dark eyes glittered. 'I made an exception to my rule for you.'

'Thank you… I think.'

'No need. The pleasure was all mine.'

It wasn't true and they both knew it. They each had their own agenda for the evening, which the other wasn't privy to, but there was no hiding the fact that the attraction smouldering between them was mutual, sexual, and lethally combustible.

Delicious as her dinner was, Genie found it difficult to swallow more than a few mouthfuls as their earlier kiss replayed on a loop in her mind. Flicking her eyes up from her plate to his face, she found him watching her again, his plate almost empty.

'Dessert?' he asked, laying his cutlery down.

She didn't want dessert, but she was far from done with Abel Kingdom. So far she'd learned barely anything. Was he an investor? Was her uncle courting him in the hope that he might save the ailing theatre with a cash injection? A sleeping partner… the idea caught her imagination and she had to make herself refocus on the business sense of the phrase.

'Coffee, maybe?' she said.

'Brandy?' he countered. Brandy was a good idea. It might loosen his tongue. Genie nodded, and then silently checked herself as her mind went in all sorts of directions at the mere thought of his tongue. She wanted him to run it down her spine.

Chapter Five

In the bar a few minutes later, Abel sat down beside Genie on the low, plump couch she'd chosen. Few customers remained, mostly couples, with the odd small group dotted here and there, their low chatter underscored by the unobtrusive pianist accompanying a smoky-voiced singer. Genie's professional eye lingered on the act, admiring the vintage ruby velvet dress worn by the vocalist.

'So, tell me what being assistant manager of a London theatre involves,' he said easily. He needed to know how much of an obstacle she was going to be, and getting her talking about her work seemed the best place to start. The knockout smile that lit her face at the mention of the theatre caught him unawares. Fuck. She loved the place even more than her goddamn uncle did.

'Everything really,' she laughed. 'I do whatever needs doing. Booking acts. Planning the seasons. Marketing. Admin.' She sipped her coffee, her eyes dancing with mischief. 'Even cleaning, sometimes.'

Abel glanced down as her knee brushed his when she moved to place her coffee cup back down on the table. He had ordered both their choices of digestif. The balance of power was equal… for the moment.

He was aware of every inch of her, and of how many inches away she was. *Too many.*

'It must get hard sometimes though? An old place like that,

a young woman like you…' he let his words tail off, the implication that she should be out enjoying the world hanging in the air between them.

'I love it,' she said, without hesitation. 'It's not just a job. It's my home. It's been in my family for generations.'

'Your home? As in you actually *live* there?'

She nodded. 'Upstairs. My uncle has one half of the top floor and I have the other.'

Shit. He knew Divine lived there, but not his niece too. Not only was he planning to buy the theatre she loved, now he was evicting her from her home too? This was getting worse. She glanced down as she accepted the brandy glass he held out, and the sweep of her exposed neck made his mouth ache to kiss it. Her hair was drawn back, a more grown up, sophisticated version of her hairstyle from earlier.

'Do you ever wear it down?' he asked, on instinct. 'Your hair?'

'Sometimes,' she murmured, and he picked up his own glass to stop his fingers from reaching for the clip that constrained her curls.

He wanted to see it down. He wanted to see it fanned out over his pillow as he fucked her.

Abel wasn't an unethical man; it bothered him that he wanted to fuck her senseless and then fuck her over. Business and pleasure, a bad mix as always. He sighed heavily. The honourable idea of letting her walk out of the hotel unscrewed pushed its way into his head, even though he fought it tooth and nail.

Genie sipped her brandy, completely thrown by his question about her hair. She'd fastened it back earlier knowing that he was less likely to place her as the burlesque dancer he'd lusted after if she kept it out of the way. Was it a wilful deception? Not exactly. She just wanted to help her uncle, and preserving her anonymity for long enough to find out what motivated Abel Kingdom was the way to do it.

'Can I ask you something, Abel?' she said, as he leaned back and placed his arm along the back of the sofa. *Did his fingertips brush against the back of her neck?* She couldn't be sure, but her jumping pulse and racing heart said yes.

'Shoot.'

Definite fingertips, stroking slow and light over her nape. Barely there, and yet it took her breath.

'Why are you interested? In our theatre, I mean?' She kept her tone as light as she could, given that the question meant so much to her.

'Shouldn't you be asking your uncle these questions?' The pad of his thumb massaged the skin beneath Genie's ear.

She tipped her head a little to the side, and he stroked the back of his fingers down her neck. Thinking was getting really, really difficult. 'Probably. But I'm asking you,' she said softly.

'Don't. Not tonight.'

'I need to know,' she said, thinking that she needed lots of things from Abel Kingdom at that very moment. This honey trap needed sweetening. She slid closer to him until her body brushed against his, drinking the last of her brandy and turning to him. He was close. So very close. And stubbornly silent.

'Are you staying here tonight?' she said, noticing the way his lips sighed apart as his dark eyes drank her in.

'Yes.'

She laid her hand on his cheek, her thumb a whisper from his lips. 'Want some company?'

Genie watched his Adam's apple move as he swallowed, and the almost painful look that flitted across his face.

'You should go home,' he said eventually, his hand still curved around her neck, his eyes asking her to stay despite the words coming out of his mouth.

The one thing she hadn't expected Abel Kingdom to do was blow hot and cold. She'd expected him to blow so hot that her skin blistered. She looked at him for a few long moments, and felt a fool when he took her hand from his face and placed his lips against the back of it for a scorching second.

'I'll walk you out,' he murmured as he stood, leaving her no option but to take the hand he offered to help her to her feet. *Business-like.* But then *not* so business like, because when he walked across the bar he kept her fingers still laced in his. It had been a long time since anyone had held Genie's hand, and the casual intimacy told her that he was fighting his urges without one hundred percent success.

Her heels clicked against the marble floor of the huge reception, and as they neared the lifts Genie stilled.

'I'll say goodnight,' she said, turning to him.

He still held her hand. 'Thank you for dinner, Abel.'

'You're welcome,' he murmured, and leaned down to kiss her cheek.

She turned her head, forcing his mouth over hers, parting her lips a little to graze him with the tip of her tongue.

He moaned low and guttural into her mouth, and in one sudden, fluid move, her back was slammed against the lift buttons as the heat of his body pressed hard into hers.

'Jesus, girl,' he cursed, his palm flat against the marble beside her head as Genie's hands smoothed down the contours of his back.

His lips opened her mouth, and the slide of his tongue over hers had her pushing her fingers into his hair to hold his head captive. Not that he was trying to escape. Quite the opposite. He had her pinned against the wall, the fire of his hard body searing hers through her dress. He kissed her as a parched man might drink water; like he couldn't stop. As if his life depended on it. The lift doors behind them slid open and he half dragged her inside the glittering, mirrored and thankfully empty chamber. As the doors closed, he pushed her against the back wall and lifted her clean off her feet, cradling her face in his hands as his crotch burned into her, hot and hard. His eyes told her that he was as far down the line as she was.

'I can't take my fucking eyes off you,' he breathed. 'Or my

hands.'

Genie didn't want him to take his hands off her. She wanted him to use them to rip her dress from her body and screw her right there against the wall of the lift.

This wasn't about his business with her uncle any more. It was about the fact that no man had ever touched her like this, made her feel like this, in her entire life. It was about the fact that this was so far beyond turned on. He made her *burn* for him, as if she were stifling and the only thing that would give her air was the orgasm he was about to give her.

'Then don't,' she said, her fingers on the buttons of his shirt. She wanted him out of it. 'Don't take your hands off me. Put them on me.'

His dark eyes glittered, and the lift juddered to a halt as his palm slammed over the emergency stop button. 'We've got three minutes before the override kicks back in,' he told her, and Genie gasped as he rucked her skirt up and slid his hand up her thigh. She had his shirt open and dragged it free of his trousers. Rock star beautiful, his hand skimmed her panties.

She was lost in how good he was. Three minutes would have to be enough. 'Put your hands all over me, Abel.'

His tongue slid between her lips as he kissed her, his fingers stroking over the silk between her legs.

'Is this where you want me to touch you, Beauty?' he whispered. *Beauty.* The endearment on his lips flipped her stomach almost as much as his touch between her legs did. 'Here?' He pushed the satin aside and ran the back of his fingers over her. His tongue traced her mouth, mirroring the sensation. So much, and still nowhere near enough.

Yes, there. Yes, more. She rocked into his fingers, moaning as they moved into her folds. Abel held her steady between his body and the wall as he opened her, explored her. 'You feel fucking amazing,' he muttered, his voice barely there, raw.

Genie clung to him, her mouth on the bunched muscles of his tanned shoulder where she'd pushed his shirt back. He was beautiful in the most masculine sense of the word. Hard. Sexy. Lava hot. And very, very turned on, if his shallow breathing pattern was anything to go on. She knew now just how much he'd been holding back downstairs. He was like a sexual force of nature. Unstoppable.

She bit down and gasped as he drew patterns on her clitoris, his mouth hot on her ear.

'I'm gonna slide my cock inside you,' he whispered, switching to a steady rhythm.

'Right here,' he pushed two fingers inside her, his thumb still working her clit. Genie cried out, opening wider, clamping her leg around his thigh. 'Beauty…' he breathed as he ran his tongue over her ear. 'Sweet Jesus…' he groaned as she rode herself against his hand.

She was going to come. He had her rapt, spiralling, grinding down on his pumping fingers. She wanted everything he had. His hands, his mouth, his cock. All of it, right here in this lift. She couldn't breathe, she was so close, so ready.

'Oh my fucking God,' she gasped, biting her lip as he slammed her harder against the wall, his mouth all over hers, his fingers knuckle deep inside her. She opened her eyes almost in shock as her orgasm started, and found his eyes open too, watching her. Dark. Lost. Possessive. Filthy. His lips parted slightly as his breath dragged out of his chest and his hips rocked against his hand between her legs. It was as close to fucking as it got. Every inch of Genie's body tensed as he crooked his fingers inside her, massaging her g-spot.

'Abel…'

He held her steady and kissed her through it. Through every dazzling, bone-melting second of her orgasm, every breathless gasp, every tremor. His lips roved over her mouth, drinking from her, connecting her to him in every way possible as her body broke hard for him.

'That was pretty fucking sexy,' he whispered a few seconds later, slowly straightening her panties and smoothing her dress over her hips before buttoning his shirt as the lift started to move again. She swallowed with difficulty as the doors slid open, unable to speak yet. Hell, she could barely stand up.

'Not our floor,' Abel mouthed against her ear, moving to stand close behind her against the wall as several people stepped into the car. A couple. A businessman. Was it obvious to them what they'd just been doing? Surely it had to be written all over her face that she'd just had the best orgasm of her life?

Abel's hand rested on her hip, and as the car began to move he drew her back and settled his still hard cock against her ass. 'How do you want it?' he spoke quietly, but Genie was pretty certain the other woman heard him. He kissed her neck slowly, sending a shudder of pleasure from her scalp to her toes. 'Like this, from behind?' he murmured as his fingers spanned her stomach, holding her against his erection as more people stepped in at the next floor. Clearly their three-minute lift stop had caused something of a backlog. It was getting a little crowded.

She all but yelped as his hand moved over her ass. 'I want you on your knees…' he whispered, and she closed her eyes. The man melted her. 'I want you on your back…' his voice was lethal in her ear. 'I want you on my cock, Beauty.'

The lift stopped again at the last but one floor and everyone except Genie and Abel stepped out of the car. As the doors slid closed, the woman turned back and flicked an appreciative glance towards Abel, and an envious one at Genie. She couldn't blame her. The man radiated sex, and right now, late night and turned on, he was the dictionary definition of hot as hell.

Abel shoved his keycard into the slot on the door, desperate to get them both the other side of it. He'd tried, he really had, but any honourable thoughts about not screwing Davey Divine's niece had taken a hike the moment that she'd turned her face into his kiss. There was something about the girl that seemed to hot-wire his cock into action, and Christ, was she responsive. The way her body had jumped when he touched her, and the look on her face when she orgasmed… he wanted to see that again and again tonight.

They tumbled into the room, a molten tangle of limbs and open mouthed kisses. He needed her naked and beneath him just about more than he'd ever needed anything from any woman in his life.

Reaching for the tie on her dress, he tugged it.

'I've wanted to do that from the moment you walked into the bar tonight,' he muttered, aware that his breathing was as ragged as hers. Her dress fell open, revealing her body to his eyes for the first time.

Abel dragged in a deep breath, stepping back enough to look at her properly.

'Fuck. Fuck, Beauty…' The sweet, full curves of her breasts beckoned him in, creamy and lush in black lace that offered her up to him like the star prize in the best quiz show on earth. Her dress fell to the floor when she shrugged, leaving her business-like image on the bedroom floor where it belonged.

It was the perfect segue from boardroom to bedroom, aside from just one thing. Abel reached for the clip in her hair and released it, drawing in a deep breath as the lush ruby waves tumbled down around her shoulders. She was breathless and siren-like, the dip of her waist calling out to his hands, the way she automatically stood with one knee slightly bent and her head a little to one side inviting him in. He shed his shirt fast, needing his skin against hers. Seeing her like this kicked his heart rate up to dangerous levels.

'Take your bra off. I want to look at you,' he whispered, tracing her lips with his tongue, trailing one finger across the warm rise and slope of her breasts. He stopped breathing when she moved back a little, a tiny smile playing over her face as she flicked first one shoulder strap off and then lifted her other delicate shoulder as if to ask him if she should do that one too.

His lips parted when she pushed it down, then reached up behind herself with a slight shimmy of her shoulders for his benefit. It worked. He couldn't take his eyes off her breasts, his anticipation sky high at the thought of seeing her naked. Once again she paused and looked at him through her lashes, and all at once, his heart lurched with unexpected familiarity.

The pieces slotted into place and Abel finally realised exactly who the stunning, confident woman in front of him was. He knew, because these were once seen, never forgotten curves. He'd willed this girl to bare her breasts once before, only back then he'd been one of hundreds in the crowd watching her strip for their approval, for their ticket money. *How? How had he not realised before?* How had his brain not connected the fucking dots?

He dropped to sit on the edge of the bed, his head in his hands, his cock still painfully hard. He'd been played. She wasn't just the deputy theatre manager and Divine's niece. And he, Abel Kingdom, didn't screw strippers or prostitutes.

'Put your fucking dress back on and get out of here, Genie.' He laid a heavy emphasis on her name.

She didn't move a muscle.

'Why does it matter what I do?' she said quietly after a full minute. He stood up with a heavy, harsh sigh, picking her dress up and shoving it towards her. Her almost bared breasts rose and fell heavily as she stared at him, wide-eyed, and it took everything he had not to throw her down on the bed and screw himself into her beautiful body until he wasn't angry any more.

Only he wasn't just angry. He was fucking furious. With her, and with himself. She had no right to wear that hurt, confused expression on her face while she stood there half naked, making him want the things he despised most of all in the world.

'It fucking matters,' he said through gritted teeth. 'Get dressed.'

This time around she did move to pick up her dress, tying it around her body with shaky fingers.

'I'm not ashamed of what I do, Abel,' she said, her voice quiet and brimming with defensive pride. 'You didn't seem to mind so much when you watched the show the other night.'

He hated that she'd seen him there. Shoving his hand into his back pocket, he pulled out a sheaf of notes.

'I don't know what you charge for a night. That ought to cover it.'

Genie stared at the money he held out for a few long seconds, and then looked back up at him again with an ocean of disgust in her clear green eyes. She knocked the notes from his fingers with the back of her hand, scattering them across the floor as she turned on her heel and left the room.

Abel sat for a long time after she'd left, mad as hell with himself. This deal was important, he needed that theatre. He could pick a building in some other part of the city, of course, but these shit end back streets represented part of his history and he wanted to claim it back.

Chapter Six

Genie couldn't face breakfast. Her uncle had left an ominously short note under her door last night asking her to come to his office at ten o'clock. It wasn't Davey's style to call official meetings; laid back conversations with coffee on the sofa usually sufficed for formalities between them.

Truth told, it wasn't just the impending meeting with her uncle that had her wound up. Abel Kingdom could claim the main prize for that. He was lucky she hadn't kneed him in the balls last night, let alone scattered his money. He had no right to pass judgement on her, nor to insult her. Gorgeous or not, he was a small-minded, arrogant suit, nothing more.

He'd seemed so much more for a little while though. Her mind drifted for the hundredth time that morning to their encounter in the lift, to the way he'd made her see stars, to the clever, filthy things he'd done with his mouth and his fingers.

At least she'd had the benefit of that incredible orgasm. She hoped he'd got the worst case of blue balls ever this morning.

A couple of minutes before ten she slipped downstairs, dressed once again in her daytime uniform of jeans and a skinny tee, Havaianas on her feet and her hair hastily plaited. Her hand stilled on the handle of the office door; should she knock? She'd never needed to before, but having found her intrusion yesterday unwelcome, she paused for thought this time and then tapped her knuckle lightly on the door before pushing it open. Her uncle looked up and smiled.

'Hi G.'

Genie closed the door and slid into the chair opposite his at the desk, noticing the unusual dark circles beneath his eyes. 'You okay? You look tired,' she said, her brows drawn together in worry.

'Not sleeping so well these days, sweetheart,' he said, patting her hand. 'There's something we need to talk about.'

Fear gripped her as she asked the question that troubled her most.

'Is it your health?'

'What? No, no. I'm fine, Genie. It's not me.'

Relief bathed Genie's fears. The idea of anything being wrong with Davey near stopped her heart.

'So if it's not you, then what is it?'

Davey sighed heavily, and Genie hated the look in his eyes. She wasn't accustomed to him wearing a troubled expression around her, he'd always protected her from fear and worry.

'It's this place, my love. The theatre.'

She swallowed, watching him closely for more information.

'It's too much, G. I can't make it work any more. Believe me, I've tried to see another way, but there just isn't one. I'm selling up.'

'Selling up? What do you mean, selling up? Uncle Davey, you can't! Theatre Divine is *ours*. It has *our* name above the door. It's our home.' She knew she sounded like a petulant child, and in that moment she felt like one. The theatre had been the only real home she'd ever known.

Her uncle still held her hand. 'I know, Gigi. I know. I don't want to let the old girl go either, but she's crippling me. The roof estimate came in a couple of weeks back and there's no way I can cover it, and the insurance won't renew unless the work's carried out. There just isn't a way around it.'

'What about the bank?'

He laughed almost wistfully. 'I love your optimism G, but

GENIE

I've already been there cap in hand. It's over two hundred grand, sweetheart. And a lot more besides if you account for all of the other work that really needs doing too. There's not a chance in hell.'

The enormity of the situation left Genie reeling.

'How long until the insurance runs out?' Her mind raced. Maybe they had six months or more to figure out a solution.

'Eight weeks.' Her uncle's downcast eyes fairly broke her heart. Two months was an impossibly short time in terms of raising the funds they needed.

They both jumped as someone knocked on the door.

'Come in, Mr Kingdom,' Davey said, quiet and resigned.

Genie whirled around in her chair as Abel walked in, brazen and clearly not as surprised to see her as she was him.

'What's *he* doing here?' She whipped her head back around to her uncle, who'd made his way around the desk and pulled up an extra chair beside Genie's.

'Have a seat,' he nodded to Abel as he settled himself back down.

'Uncle Davey?' Genie laid both hands on the table.

'Genie. Mr Kingdom wants to buy the theatre.'

'Like hell he does!' she half yelled, turning her eyes on him at last. 'No way. No fucking way.'

'Genie!' Shocked by her language in front of their visitor, her uncle admonished her in a tone he hadn't had to use since she'd been a child. She turned to him with an apology, but no less passion in her eyes.

'I'm sorry, but you can't be serious. You'd sell this place to him? For what?' As she said it, realisation dawned and she swung back round to face Abel. 'You want to turn this into one of your gym palaces?'

He nodded. 'It's ideal.'

'No! No. Uncle Davey, please.' Tears stung her eyes at the idea of her beloved home being ripped apart. 'Surely there's another way here? Someone else we can talk to, an investor who

45

would at least keep the theatre going?'

'Genie, do you think I haven't tried?' he said gently, his eyes full of love and compassion.

'Then let *me* try,' she said, clutching at straws for a stay of execution.

'Sweetheart, there's nothing you can do.'

Even as he spoke, the idea formed in her mind. 'Eight weeks. You said we had eight weeks. Let me try, Uncle Davey. Please… give me eight weeks to raise the money.'

Abel cleared his throat. 'Never gonna happen.'

'I wasn't asking you,' Genie shot back at him, hating him enough to wish the crumbling roof would fall in on his head.

Abel shrugged. 'There's no way in hell that you're gonna raise that kind of money.' He turned to her uncle. 'I'm not an unreasonable man, Mr Divine, I can see you've got some… *family issues* to handle here.' He eyed Genie, emphasising the phrase *family issues* as if she were a troublesome teenager. 'It'll take my legal team six weeks or so to organise the necessary surveys and raise the sales paperwork anyway. Eight weeks, and then you sign on the dotted line and this place is mine.'

He reached out his hand over the desk, and Genie watched her uncle nod gravely and accept the terms of Abel Kingdom's offer.

'Eight weeks' grace, and unless Genie can work a miracle, then I'll sign your papers.'

Abel nodded. 'And the apartment?'

Genie's eyes flickered between the two men. She really didn't like the look on her uncle's face.

'From Friday, as promised,' he said, pushing a set of keys across the desk.

His business apparently concluded to his satisfaction, Abel pushed his chair back as he stood up, pocketing the keys as he went.

'Pleasure doing business with you, Mr Divine,' he said, shaking Davey's hand for a second time as he left. At the doorway, he turned back.

'You'd better start rubbing that lamp and asking for your three wishes,' he said, his eyes on Genie. 'Because the way I see it, that's the only thing that's gonna save you now.' He touched his fingers to his forehead in mock salute, the light of challenge bright in his dark eyes as he turned and left.

Genie turned slowly back to her uncle, the room suddenly huge and empty without Abel Kingdom's overwhelming presence in it.

'What did he mean, the apartment?'

Even before Davey spoke, Genie knew she wasn't going to like the answer.

'He's taking over my apartment from Friday.'

'Your apartment *here*, upstairs?'

Davey ran a worried hand over his thinning hair. 'Genie, you have to understand that none of this is what I want either. I love this place just as much as you do, but it's too late. I told him he could move in here from Friday, he has business in London and needs a base for a few months. I was planning to move in with Robin after the sale anyway. I've just brought things forward by a few weeks.'

'So what am I supposed to do? Live here under the same roof as him for the next two months?'

'I know it's not ideal, G. What could I say?'

'Err, no?' Genie tried unsuccessfully to keep bitter sarcasm out of her voice. 'You could have said no!'

'I couldn't really, could I? Because believe it or not Genie, Abel Kingdom is actually our only hope.'

Genie galvanised herself into action back in her upstairs apartment half an hour later. Her uncle might have given up the fight, but she was only just getting started. Abel Kingdom was *so* not their only hope. Eight weeks might not be the most workable of timescales, but everything she loved in the world was at stake and she wasn't going down without the mother of all fights.

Coffee in one hand, she opened her door to let Deanna in. She'd called her friend the moment she'd left Davey's office, rallying the troops for battle. This wasn't just her fight, it was all of the theatre staff whose jobs were in peril, which included Deanna.

She listened in horrified silence as Genie outlined the meeting she'd just endured.

'Shit, G. Eight weeks? What the hell can we do in that time?' Deanna pushed her dark hair behind her ears, tapping a pencil on the pad in front of her on the coffee table. The sheet of paper was frighteningly blank.

'We need something special. Something that'll really pull in the crowds,' Genie said.

'Well, you've been the biggest draw by far since you started performing here,' Deanna said.

It was true; since Genie's return from her year on stage at the Moulin Rouge in Paris twelve months previously, her twice-weekly shows had been consistent sell outs. Other cabarets and shows had proved hit and miss with the fickle public, but Genie's burlesque show was a winner every time.

She nodded slowly, acknowledging the truth behind Deanna's words.

'Sex sells, that's for sure,' she said, clicking her tongue against the roof of her mouth, deep in thought. 'Fine. So we'll sell sex.'

She rolled her eyes at Deanna's raised eyebrows. 'Not *actual* sex. Call it what you like. Titillation. Excitement.' Standing up, she paced the floor with her coffee cup cradled in her hands. 'Either way, I mean more burlesque. A troupe. And not just twice a week, like now. Every night if we need to. And matinees.' She was talking faster now, gripped by the hope in the idea. 'I think the demand's there. We know it is. You just said so yourself.'

She turned to Deanna, whose pencil was flying over the paper. That was a good sign. Deanna in planning mode was a force to be reckoned with.

'The Divine Girls,' she suggested trying the name out, then writing it down. 'I like that. How about trying to get an investor on board?'

Genie nodded. 'I've no idea who or how, but yes.'

Deanna scribbled a few words and then looked up. 'I don't suppose Stud-muffin could be persuaded to switch sides?'

Genie almost laughed at how far off the mark Deanna was. 'He thinks I'm a prostitute.'

Deanna gave a contemptuous snort. 'That wasn't what his face told me when he watched the show the other night.'

'Yeah, well, things changed. I met him for dinner.'

'You did?' Her friend placed the pencil down, wide-eyed. 'Spill.'

Genie dropped down into the chair opposite and shrugged. 'We had dinner.'

'Yeah, we established that much already. And?'

'We… we talked.'

'And?'

Genie knew what her friend was angling for. 'He hadn't realised I was the same girl he'd watched perform.'

'Ah.' Deanna picked up her coffee. 'At what point did he realise?'

'Mm. About midway?'

'Midway through what?' Deanna asked. 'Dinner, or sex?'

'Jeez, Dee! Fine. Midway between shoving his hand down my knickers and unbuttoning his trousers. Is that clear enough for you?'

Deanna whistled and puffed her fringe out of her eyes.

'Was he as good as he looked?'

'Dee. The man tried to pay me for sex. He's a chauvinist Australian pig.'

'He's Australian?'

'Yes, but the more important point of that sentence was that he's a vile pig, okay?'

'Totally.' Deanna nodded. 'Totally. It's just… it sounds like things got pretty far, considering he's a vile pig. A bloody good looking one though.'

'He was fine until he realised who I was, and then he freaked. Jekyll and Hyde. Thrust money at me.'

Deanna smiled dreamily. 'I wish someone would do that to me.'

'Seriously Dee, I'm not kidding. He practically threw me out of his room.'

'And he's moving in across the hall from you on Wednesday?'

Genie nodded.

Deanna grinned and touched her mug against Genie's.

'Then on behalf of women everywhere, let's give him hell.'

Chapter Seven

Abel looked around his new home, already wondering if he'd made the right decision moving into Davey Divine's apartment. It was eclectic, its furnishings far bolder than suited Abel's tastes. He'd made the arrangements whilst under the impression that the sale would proceed immediately, and on reflection he could have given Divine the option to stay in residence until the end of the eight weeks' grace period.

He could have, but he hadn't done, because for all the wrong reasons, he now wanted to take up residence in the flat opposite Genie.

He wanted to be opposite her to piss her off.

He wanted to be opposite her to keep an eye on her.

He wanted to be opposite her to stamp his authority all over the place.

He wanted to be opposite her because he was intrinsically drawn to her as he'd never been to a woman before.

She'd looked so fragile and young the other day in her flip flops and plaits, different from the woman he'd almost screwed the other night, and a world away from the stage siren he'd watched twist the audience around her little finger. She was an enigma, so many women in one. Fascinating, and he already hated that she occupied so much of his headspace. He couldn't even be sure which of her many faces turned him on. He wanted it to be the barefaced girl in jeans, and warred against the way his cock hardened at the memory of how she'd looked up on stage.

He didn't want to want that woman, that dangerously powerful, knowing siren. He didn't want to want Genie Divine at all.

Maybe it was always meant to be this way back here. A woman like her, in a place like this. Was that why he'd come here? To prove a point, to slay his demons so he could finally sleep easy at night?

It was just that he hadn't expected one of his demons to be temptation in the form of a red haired harlot who lived across the hallway.

He frowned as the low, thumping bass beat of rock music started to reverberate through the building. What was going on? It was barely midday. Surely the theatre wasn't open yet? Taking the two flights of stairs down to the ground floor at some pace, he opened the door into the auditorium and found himself confronted by a dark haired girl with a camera slung around her neck and a clipboard in her hand.

'I take it you're not here to audition?' she said, eying him coolly.

'Audition for what?' Abel asked, his eyes moving over her shoulder into the busy foyer behind, the throng of people – almost exclusively women in various states of undress. This was turning into an interesting morning.

'The Divine Girls.'

'The what?' Abel heard what the girl had said, but his brain didn't process the words because Genie had just appeared through the same door as he had a few seconds before. She caught sight of him at the same moment, her bright eyes on fire with challenge.

'Come to watch the show again?' she said defiantly, as she approached.

'I wasn't impressed enough to see it twice,' Abel said. Deanna laughed softly and turned her face away, knowing better.

He gestured towards the other room. 'What's going on in there?'

'And that's your business because…?'

'Anything that happens from here on in is my business, Genie.'

'Not for the next eight weeks it isn't. Not ever, if I get my way.'

'Which you won't.'

Deanna cleared her throat beside them.

'Auditions start in three minutes G. Twenty-three applicants so far, some really promising ones.'

Genie rubbed her friend's arm. 'That's even better than I'd hoped. I'll be through in a sec, okay?'

Abel's eyes flickered over Genie as she spoke to her friend. Denim hot pants over black footless tights, a cropped, black long sleeved tee that clung to the lines of her body. She had a dancer's grace and a stripper's curves. It was a shit hot combination to which, despite his best intentions, his body reacted every single time she was in the same room. She'd tied that unmissable red hair up on top of her head and had her arms folded over her chest, her chin jutting out antagonistically as she turned back to him once they were alone.

'These are closed auditions. You might live upstairs, but that doesn't give you open access down here too.'

'You don't get to tell me what I can do here. Access all areas. If I want to come and watch your little exercise class, I'll sit right down and watch.'

'It's not a goddamn exercise class,' she spat back, biting as he'd hoped she would. 'This theatre's going burlesque, full time as of right now. With its own troupe. Nightly shows. Matinees even, if there's a call for it.'

Abel half laughed. 'Put your leg warmers away, green eyes. This isn't the Kids from Fame. This is real life, and in two months this place will be mine.'

'Over my dead body,' she said, her eyes blazing. 'Or preferably, over yours.'

He could tell she meant it with every fibre of her being. 'Why don't you just let it go, Beauty?' he asked, surprising himself more than Genie. He'd intended his words to come out as scathing, not gentle. He saw her jaw work as she swallowed, confusion narrowing her eyes for a second as she slowly shook her head.

'And make it easy for you to rip the heart right out of my home?' she said, and he didn't miss the emotion that thickened her voice. 'Go to hell, Kingdom.'

She stalked away from him into the auditorium, leaving him feeling as if she'd somehow claimed victory in that particular battle. Not that it mattered, because dance troupe or no dance troupe, she didn't stand a chance of winning the war.

Genie glanced up at the clock later that afternoon. It was a little before four, a few hours until she was due on stage for her second time as the Genie of the Lamp. Performance days always set her nerves into a pleasurable jangle, a heady anticipation that made her pulse quicken and her heart bang. She loved being out there on stage, more brave and powerful and unafraid than she was day to day. Right now, she needed those feelings more than ever, because none of those adjectives seemed to apply to her regular life.

Knowing that her Uncle Davey wasn't just across the hall any more felt as if someone had ripped away her comfort blanket, and knowing that Abel Kingdom was there instead felt as if someone had rigged her safe sanctuary with a grid of trip wires. The man confused the hell out of her, and the fact that he was outlandishly beautiful made it far harder not to fall into his traps. How could it be that her head hated him and her body wanted him?

He'd called her Beauty again earlier, and it had sounded even more intimate in the midst of their disagreement. Almost as if he hadn't intended to say it at all. She'd been tempted to call him on it, yet she hadn't, because somewhere deep inside she thrilled to it. Calling him on it might mean he didn't say it again.

Was she so easily seduced? She wouldn't have said so before the arrival of her antipodean neighbour. How the hell was she supposed to sleep tonight knowing that he was sleeping under the same roof?

Shaking her head, she headed for her bedroom, shedding her clothes as she went. Ritual formed a big part of performance day, and Genie's particular ritual involved an afternoon rest to steady her mind before showering and heading down to her dressing room to begin preparations. She kept the two parts of her life consciously separate: downstairs she was Genie the showgirl with her stage make-up and rhinestone-encrusted costumes, while upstairs she kept her civvy clothes and private belongings.

She'd decorated her apartment with thrift shop bargains and vintage furniture from flea markets, serene and feminine in a neutral palette of ivories and greys with nude pink and palest lavender accessories. The bleached-out floorboards and tall windows lent the space the ambience of a New York loft, while the large, ivory and glass chandelier added a dash of opulent glamour. Genie adored the whole place, from her big brass bed to the overstuffed couches with their velvet cushions. It was a distinctly female lair, and a direct and purposefully peaceful contrast to the bright feathers and sparkling sequins of her on-stage persona.

Naked, she lay down on the bed, sighing with pleasure as the plump, dull silver silk eiderdown gathered her in. Being positioned at the top of the building made for warmth in the winter, and stifling heat in the summer. Right now it was just about perfect, the late May sunlight shafting in through the high windows and warming Genie's skin and the room around her. She closed her eyes and breathed in deeply through her nose. In. And out. In, and out. Concentrating her thoughts on her breathing, she let her limbs go heavy on the bed and relaxed for what felt like the first time since she'd laid eyes on Abel Kingdom on Sunday evening. She was warm, and oh so comfortable, and pleasurably drifting towards sleep.

And *that* was when the music started. Loud, thumping music

coming from across the hall. Her uncle had always been a considerate neighbour; it seemed that Abel wasn't similarly inclined. She snapped her eyes open and sat up. Did he realise she was up here too? Was he goading her? If he was, it was working.

She swung her feet down and grabbed her robe from the hook on the back of the door. As she tied the sash belt, the dove grey silk of her robe - an opulent and much loved birthday gift from her uncle - swished pleasurably around her ankles. Tracking barefoot across the hallway, she rapped her knuckles against the door.

He didn't hear her, probably because his music was so damn loud, so she banged again, only harder.

He swung the door wide a couple of seconds later. His eyes swept down her robe to her pink painted toes and then back up to her face as he lounged against the doorframe with his arms folded over his chest.

'Come to invite me to a pyjama party?' His tone was insolently mocking.

How did he have the knack for making her instantly furious? Genie swallowed down the words she'd really have liked to say and tried to arrange her face into a polite smile.

'Could you please turn down your music? I'm trying to sleep in there.' She jerked her head towards her own door.

'Sorry,' he frowned, clearly intent on winding her up. 'I can't hear you. Music's too loud.' She watched him head back into the apartment to turn the volume down, wishing she had something to throw at him and trying not to notice the way his faded jeans sat on his hips or the hard-muscled outline of his shoulders through his tee shirt.

'Is this what you do in the afternoons around here?' he said when he returned a few seconds later.

She arched her eyebrows at him. 'Meaning?'

'You, prancing around in your nightie and harping on about my music. Is this gonna happen every afternoon?'

'I just need a little bit of quiet on performance days. That's all.'

'You're performing tonight?' Genie saw the flare in his eyes that he didn't hide quickly enough.

'Yes.'

'With the lamp?'

What was this? 'Yes. Why? Want a front row seat?'

He pushed a hand through his dark hair and laughed softly at her, and Genie's treacherous gaze flickered to the band of tanned skin exposed beneath the hem of his shirt.

'No thanks. Seen one stripper, you've seen 'em all.'

'I'm not a stripper. And while we're on the subject, I'm not a prostitute either.'

'You justify it to yourself however you like, darlin'. Whatever helps you sleep at night.'

'I'm not justifying myself, to you or anyone else. I'm damn proud of what I do,' she retorted furiously.

He nodded. 'Figures. Go get your beauty sleep, then.'

The look on his face told her that she was wasting her breath arguing the point with him any more at that moment. She'd got what she wanted; he'd turned the music down.

'Thank you,' she muttered, her eyes flashing as she turned away. As she pushed her own door open, he spoke again, very quietly.

'You work what your mamma gave you while you still can, Beauty, because one day you'll be old and no one will want to watch you take your clothes off any more. You ever wondered what happens to strippers when they're past their sell by date?'

She turned back angrily, and the look on his face chilled her bones.

'Just what the hell is your problem, Abel?'

He shrugged and held his hands wide. 'No problems here.'

'Liar. You hate what I do. Tell me why.'

He shook his head, his face shutting down her enquiry, changing tack smoothly. 'About that pyjama party...' His eyes moved over her body. 'I don't own any.'

That game again. Chicken.

'Good. Me neither,' she said. 'I sleep naked.'

'Think about me while you're lying there, baby,' he murmured silkily with the ghost of a wink.

'I need sleep, not nightmares,' she shot back, then slammed her door before he had a chance to say anything more or notice how her nipples had stiffened beneath the thin silk of her robe.

Abel closed his door and leaned his head back against it. *Genie fucking Divine.* The girl was killing him with her bravado and her naked afternoon naps. She hadn't closed her door anywhere near fast enough for him not to see her nipples standing proud against her robe. Were they still stiff now? Had she taken that robe off to lie down naked on her bed again? He'd seen neither her bedroom nor her naked body, but his imagination had no trouble filling in the gaps. White cotton sheets… Red hair flung out over her pillows… Rose pink, puckered nipples just begging to be sucked…

Fuck. He needed a cold shower.

Genie leaned against her closed door, her hand on her throat as her heart hammered. *Abel fucking Kingdom.* The man was killing her with his blinkered views and smart mouth. *Christ, he had an amazing mouth.* Lush, full and sexy. She hated the words that came out of it, yet still she couldn't stop herself from imagining it all over her body. What was he doing over there right this minute? She walked slowly back through her apartment, shedding her robe once more and settling on her bed in the quiet, sun-warmed room.

Closing her eyes, she tried to concentrate on her breathing again, to recapture her earlier peace. Breathe in. Breathe out. In. Out.

The movement of her rib cage lifted her breasts and her fingers settled lightly over them, testing their soft fullness in her palms with a sigh. Her nipples ached, still stiff for the dark-eyed man across the hall. How would his mouth feel on them? Her fingers tightened on her nipples at the thought, and she arched instinctively into his imaginary hold. Would he cup her breasts in his big tanned hands while he kissed them? Would he lick her nipples slowly, or suck them hard into the heat of his mouth? Genie couldn't suppress a moan, her hands full of her own flesh, her head full of images of Abel's dark head bent over her. He was shirtless, and she could see his mouth closing over her nipple as he knelt between her thighs on the bed…

Abel stepped under the shower, glad that Davey Divine had expensive tastes in plumbing. The powerful jet of water sluiced over his head, and he turned his face up into the fierce spray as the water soaked down his body. Genie lingered behind his closed eyes, her body still naked against her sheets, her nipples still stiff and waiting for his attention. She'd be soft, and warm, and she'd exude that same clean, irresistible scent that she'd tasted of in the lift the other night. His cock stiffened at the memory, and his hand moved involuntarily down the wetness of his torso to wrap around his erection. Fuck, he'd been two minutes away from screwing her.

Was she sleeping now? He imagined her cheeks flushed, her body bared and spread on the bed. Would she hear him if he opened her door now and went to her? Would she wake if he stood beside her bed and watched her sleep? His hand slid along the solid length of his cock as he conjured the length of her nude body in his head. The fullness of her tits, begging to be sucked. The subtle outline of her ribcage, the slopes and curves of her stomach, the feminine swell of her hips. He leaned back against the tiles in the shower enclosure with a low moan. Would her legs be closed, or splayed? *Splayed*. In Abel's mind at least, they were, one knee bent out on the sheets to let him see between them, inviting him closer…

Genie's hands moved over her body, imagining Abel's doing the same. His mouth, hot and open on her neck. The hard weight of his body over hers. She opened her legs as her hand moved between them, remembering how amazing he'd been in the lift the other night. The way his fingers had opened her, explored her... Her own fingers moved into the slickness, wet for him now as she'd been wet for him then. Jesus, he'd been good. He'd had the measure of her in seconds, fast and filthy one moment, slow and seductive the next. Genie pushed her shoulders back into the mattress as she spread her legs wider and touched herself, her breath coming in short gasps as her fingers worked. He'd used his thumb, flat like this... he'd slid his fingers inside her, like that... Genie lifted her hips into her hand, greedy for the beginnings of her orgasm as it sizzled in her veins. She needed him now, here, she wanted him naked between her thighs, filling her right there... she crooked her fingers inside her body, groaning, massaging herself as he had, her other hand working her clit... oh God... Abel... so good, so much... Genie gasped, her forehead damp and her teeth clenched, right on the delicious edge... make me come, Abel... please make me come...

Abel moaned, pumping his hand over his shaft harder at the thought of Genie's splayed legs. Fuck, he wanted to bury his head between them, to lick her inner thighs, to open her folds wide with his fingers until he could see her clit begging for him to lower his mouth over it... he could feel the swell of it against his tongue, feel her fingers gripping his hair when he licked her. Christ, he was so hard it was painful. He rubbed himself faster, the water drumming his face as he tipped his head back to rest against the tiles. He could almost hear her moaning his name, feel her like hot silk in his hands as he pushed her knees wider apart, the friction, the delicious tightness of fucking into her body as she bucked under him. A ragged gasp. *Genie.* Her nails raking down his back. Fuck... fuck... *oh fucking hell yes.* Abel's knees almost buckled as his hips jerked, the sensation too fierce to hold it back any more. His orgasm slammed him back against the wall as he came in hot, hard bursts over the clenched muscles of his stomach, one arm flung over his eyes, his bottom lip caught between his teeth so tightly it hurt.

Genie clamped her thighs around her hands, gasping to breathe through the pleasurable intensity of the second best orgasm of her life. Christ, she was shaking. Afterwards, as her heart banged in her chest, she pulled the softness of her eiderdown over her body and closed her eyes, not even trying to make sense of what was happening to her when it came to the off-the-scale hot Australian across the hallway.

Abel washed his body clean as the lust ebbed, cursing Genie for making him want her, and cursing himself for thinking that coming back to England had ever been a good idea.

Chapter Eight

Trying to concentrate on work with a full scale theatre production going on two floors below proved too much of a challenge for Abel a few hours later. Davey Divine was on stage down there, warming up the crowd for Genie, their laughter almost shaking the rafters that Abel's apartment rested amongst. He rooted through Divine's cupboards, on the hunt for headphones to attempt to drown out the noise, and returned to the table with a bottle of Jack Daniels and a tumbler to drown his sorrows instead. At least the man had decent taste in liquor, Abel reflected sourly as he poured a drinker's measure into the bottom of the glass.

He closed his laptop. The noise levels made work nigh on impossible, and the knowledge that Genie was due on stage soon had him restless. There were a million and one careers she could have chosen to pursue. Why did she have to choose *this* one? Why would any woman choose to take her clothes off for money when she had other options? He knocked back half of the whisky, closing his eyes as the hit of heat and spice warmed his throat.

What kind of guys did she think sat out there watching her? Decent men? Potential dates? Because Abel knew better. He knew better, because he'd grown up around this scene, or else a grubbier, less glittery version of it. A child in a very grown up world, he'd seen things no child should ever have to see and he'd heard things no child should ever have to hear. Genie was wrong to defend the world she chose to live in. It attracted low lifes and no-hopers, and her inability to see that told him all he needed to know about her.

The slide of trumpets ratcheted up and thunderous applause told Abel that showtime had arrived for the star turn downstairs. He slugged back the rest of the whisky and refilled his glass, cradling it in his hands as the sultry music drifted around his ears. Closing his eyes, he could almost see her down there now, her body appearing out of that glittering lamp for them all to feast their eyes on.

Scraping his chair back, he paced the floor. He should leave, get out of the building until the show was over. He made for the door, not even registering that the whisky was still in his hands until he reached the bottom of the stairs and opened the door that led directly into the side of the stalls. There was no need for him even to look at the stage. He could make his way around the back of the auditorium and out into the street to suck down clean night air. It was what he told himself, even though he wasn't ever destined to get further than the doorway at the bottom of the stairs. It was a perfect vantage point from which to view the stage, and he was a lost cause as soon as he set eyes on Genie up there on the stage.

Leaning his shoulder against the doorframe, he folded his arms over his chest and rested his head on the wood with a sigh that sat somewhere between frustration and longing. She was utterly fucking stunning. Still in the early stages of her act, peeling off her long gloves, throwing glances over her shoulder at the crowd, the sweet curves of her ass turning on every man in the place.

This wasn't the spunky girl he'd argued with earlier. This wasn't the sensual woman he'd fantasised about in the shower, either. This was Genie the consummate showgirl, a woman of the world with a killer body and no morals.

Which was real? How could the same woman have so many faces? And how could they all be beautiful in their own way? She beguiled him even though he didn't want her to, she made him want to be the guy who screwed her when she came off that stage tonight. Her fingers moved to unlace her corset and he wanted to do it for her, to strip her for his private pleasure rather than see her offer herself to this paying, excited crowd. His eyes moved over the shadowed faces watching her, all of them willing her to take everything off for their titillation. Men. Women. Turned on, every last one of them.

What thoughts ran through their minds? Were these well dressed women wishing they looked even half as good as Genie, or were they imagining themselves up there as the centre of attention? Were they jealous that their husbands wanted her? Or maybe they wanted her too, were looking at Genie's beautiful curves and wondering how she'd feel in their hands. It was easier to guess at the thoughts filling the heads of the men sitting in the audience. Right about now they'd be willing Genie to turn around and show them her tits, waiting for her to go further, to look their way as she slipped her panties off. They'd be shifting in their seats to accommodate their hardening cocks, imagining themselves fucking Genie over that lamp. He knew because he'd had those same thoughts when he'd watched her show - he didn't delude himself that they were original. And now, despite the fact that he hated it with every inch of his being, he was having them all over again.

Genie peeled her corset off, and he held his breath until she turned around and let him see her breasts. Knowing that he'd made this woman come filled him with fierce pride; he wanted to tell every other man in the place. To make them *burn* with jealousy.

Fuck. What was she doing to him? He threw the whisky down the back of his throat, hating himself for being no better than the paying audience, for being as bad as the men who'd watched his mother strip all those years ago with those same feral instincts driving their actions.

Would these people go home tonight and think of Genie as

they fucked their wives? Or would they hang around, hoping to catch a glimpse of her at the stage door? Did they harbour dark, lustful ideas of dragging her down some filthy alley and shoving notes down her bra as they forced themselves on her?

Looking back at Genie, he rubbed his hand over the back of his neck, too hot even though he wore only a tee shirt. The girl had incredible tits. He'd been so close to seeing them the other night, to glimpsing her nipples, and he'd stopped her. How had he found the strength to do that? Right at that moment he had no clue, because the only thought in his head was how much he wanted her to take off those tassels and let him see her no doubt pink and perfect buds. Every last inch of her creamy skin glittered as she lay back over the lamp, and he wanted to go up there and lay his body over hers, hide her from everyone else's eyes and feel her curves pliant beneath him.

Her act was drawing to a close now. She sat upright on top of the lamp, and, as she reached for those itty-bitty tassels right before the lights went down, she turned his way and looked him straight in the eye.

Fuck. Had she known he was there all along? He backed up, breathless, closing the door and standing in the shaded stairwell as she took her bows to rapturous applause and cheering.

Minutes passed, and beyond the door he could hear the sounds of the evening winding down. The dwindling chatter of the crowd, the laughter of a woman, the rustle of coats. He heard it all as he stood, and after a while he made his way along the corridor, past the staircase, and out of the stage door at the rear of the building.

The dark skies overhead held no stars when he leaned back against the rough bricks and looked up. Or perhaps it was that the lights of the city obscured them from his view. He longed suddenly for home, for the fresh air and wide, star-studded Australian skies. This place wasn't for him, these people were not for him. He'd come here hoping for resolution, and instead he'd found himself conflicted, a night watchman for a woman he didn't understand.

He'd never been much of a smoker, yet in that moment, with one foot braced against the wall, he really wished he had a cigarette.

In her dressing room, Genie wrapped a slippery green silk robe around her body and sat still, drinking in the silence, thinking of Abel watching her tonight. He was so goddamn contrary; hell-bent on hating strippers, yet the look on his face had told her how much he'd enjoyed the show. Who was he trying to kid? Himself, or her? And why did it even matter to him so much? Jesus, it was theatre, a show designed to please and to tease, nothing more and nothing less. Sexy, harmless fun.

His overreaction to the performance made her crazy, his determination to make it - and her – into something seedy charged her with anger. He was filling her head once again for all the wrong reasons. She needed to centre her thoughts on saving the theatre from him, not on proving herself to him as a woman.

Tiredness stole over her bones. She needed her cosy pyjamas and her bed, and unusually, she decided to head upstairs and award herself the luxury of bathing in her apartment bathroom rather than down in the shower cubicle of her dressing room. The big old theatre felt a lonely place tonight. Maybe it was the fact that her uncle wasn't around any more, but she found that she wanted the comfort of closing her own front door more than she wanted to avoid getting glitter in her bathtub.

Tying the belt of her robe, she let herself out of the dressing room and made her way upstairs, without a thought for the keys she'd left downstairs in her bag until she was on the top floor and found herself unable to open her door.

Crap. She didn't want to go all the way back down again. She leaned her backside on the table that stood beneath the landing skylight, taking care not to knock over the lamp set there to cast a warm creamy glow over their living space.

She glanced towards Abel's door, her mind spinning. There was a spare key to her door on Abel's key ring, not that he knew it. She had a key to his door on her set too, not that he knew that either. She and her uncle had kept a spare for each other so they could come and go as they pleased, flopping on each other's sofas for a cuppa and a gossip. She hadn't given a thought to the fact that Abel had her door key until now, and now that she had, she wanted it back.

Should she knock on his door then? She wasn't worried about waking him. He'd looked far from ready to sleep when she'd seen him a little while back. As she stood there and deliberated, the sound of his footsteps jogging up the creaky stairs took the decision from her hands.

He appeared on the landing a few seconds later, his dark eyes flickering down the length of her legs exposed by the robe. The lamplight turned his skin burnished gold and deepened his thick, dark hair to almost black.

'If you're hanging around to tout for business, I'm not interested.'

The bastard. Genie went from tired to red-hot furious in a heartbeat.

'Fuck off, Abel. I've just about had it with your smart wise cracks. I don't judge you, and you have no right to judge me either.'

He shrugged insolently. 'Just tellin' it like it is, darlin.'

She hated him. Hated him calling her darlin' in that derisory way. Wanted him to call her Beauty in that sexy way again. Hated him for making her want to hear him say it again.

'You don't fool me for a second, Abel Kingdom. You enjoyed the show tonight.'

He turned away from her towards his door, his laugh harsh. 'In your dreams, baby.'

'In yours, more like,' she said, trying not to think about the fact that he had been the star of her bedroom fantasies that very afternoon. 'I saw the look on your face tonight. You were no different to anyone else out there watching the show.'

He stilled, the muscles of his back working beneath his tee shirt. 'You're wrong,' he said levelly.

'And you're lying,' she countered even more quietly. He turned around. 'Why, Abel? Why won't you admit that you enjoyed it?'

He stepped towards her into the amber pool of light thrown by the lamp, towering over her as she stood in her bare feet. Up close, he was a broad-chested, menacing man, yet she knew with certainty that she didn't need to fear him physically. He stared down at her, and she watched his eyes as he decided what to say next. She saw him swallow, watched raw emotion flash across his face, and the nerve that jumped in his cheek as he clenched his teeth. He was a man battling with himself, and she wanted to know what drove him.

'I don't need to explain myself to you,' was all that he said. 'Go to bed.'

His shutters slammed down again. She practically saw them falling over his eyes.

'I've left my keys downstairs,' she said. 'There's a spare in your set.'

He frowned, fishing his keys out of his jeans. 'I have a key to your door?'

'You did, until now,' she corrected. 'I'll have it back, please.'

'Do you have one for my door?'

Genie sighed. 'Yes.'

'Then you can have yours back when I have mine.'

He really was a world class wind-up, and her temper flared. 'Stop being a dick and give me my key, Abel.'

He flicked through the keys and identified the one for Genie's door, then stepped forward and slid it into the lock.

'Don't call me names when I'm helping you out,' he admonished her silkily.

She half laughed at the absurdity of his statement. 'You're not helping me. You're trying to take everything I have. Believe me, I've called you far, far worse in my head. Be glad you only heard dick and liar.'

'I haven't lied to you, Beauty,' he said, after a heartbeat, his hand still on the keys in the door. 'Not once.'

'You're lying to yourself too if you believe that, Abel,' she said, her words softened by his term of endearment. 'I saw you the first time you came here. You were turned on watching me on stage. And again, watching me tonight.'

'You're dead wrong,' he muttered, his eyes nailed to her door. He was close to her, and she could almost feel the anger contained in his taut body.

She wasn't wrong and she knew it, and she sensed that this went to the core of him. Reaching out, she placed a hand on his chest and saw him close his eyes in silent resistance.

'Is it so bad to be turned on by me like this, Abel?' she said, feeling his heart beating hard against her palm.

'Don't fuck with me, Genie,' he ground out, pushing her door open. 'I mean it.'

It was one of those moments when sense goes out the window and instinct takes over. Genie tugged at the belt of her robe and shrugged it off, letting it fall to the floor in one fluid motion, revealing her body in nothing but the nipple tassels and tiny crystal g-string she'd left the stage wearing.

'Is it so bad to want me when I look like this, Abel?'

He turned towards her and dropped his eyes, his palms scrubbing over his jaw as if he didn't trust his hands if they weren't occupied.

'I told you not to fuck with me, Beauty,' he breathed, almost agonised, and she saw the exact, dangerous moment that his resolve snapped.

He shoved the keys into his pocket and then his hands were on her waist, lifting her up onto the hallway table, sending the lamp flying as he parted her thighs with his hip to let him in between them. Genie gasped when he tipped her chin back with his hand and dipped his head to her throat, the erotic drag of his hot and open mouth down her skin. The clean, aromatic scent of his hair surrounded her, dark silk falling over his brow as a low, animalistic growl rattled through his chest.

Genie put her hands on either side of his stubbled jaw and lifted his head to hers, desperate for his kiss yet still shocked by the intensity of it when he finally gave it to her. Hard enough to bruise, designed to punish, profoundly sexy. She gulped down air and dragged his head down again when he lifted it, his crotch hard in hers as he clamped her against him with his hand splayed on her back, his other hand cupping the back of her neck. He held her as a man holds a woman he adores, and he kissed her as a man kisses a woman he needs to fuck more than he needs to breathe.

Her hands moved under the bottom of his tee shirt, and he broke off for the briefest of seconds to drag it over his head before pulling her into him again, skin to skin. The sensation blindsided her; the heat and the beauty of him. Tanned deep bronze in the way that only a man who spends his life out in the sunshine can be, with a fine trail of dark hair traced on his midriff that she wanted to follow all the way down into his jeans. His hands move to cover and cup her breasts, making her moan into his mouth.

'I warned you not to fuck with me…' he muttered again, still angry even as his mouth gentled over her jaw, grazing the skin beneath her ear, drifted over her collarbones to the swell of her breasts in his hands, somehow lewder for the scant cover provided by the crystal tassels than if she'd been naked.

'You're covered in fucking glitter,' he spoke against her skin as he dragged her hips forward to the edge of the table and trailed his tongue over the top curves of her breasts. 'You too,' she whispered, smoothing her fingers over the gold dust that had transferred itself onto his shoulders, his cheekbones, his abs.

She drew in a shuddering breath when Abel lowered his head and licked around the edges of the sequinned tassels. No man had ever touched her in costume like this before. Having his mouth slide around the tassels was just about the sexiest thing she'd ever seen or felt, and her body screamed for his tongue over her nipples.

'Take these off,' he said, tugging lightly on the tasselled ends, his restless mouth roaming the curves her breasts. 'I need to taste all of you.'

Genie groaned with frustration, wanting him to see her too. 'They don't come off easily.'

Abel grumbled low in his chest, like an animal denied his dinner. Genie understood; she wanted him to feast on her just as much.

'And this?' he said, bending to kiss his way down her stomach and lick along the top edge of the crystal g-string. 'Is this welded on too?'

She shook her head, although he hadn't waited for her reply in any case. He'd already dropped to his haunches, his fingers splayed on her inner thighs, holding her open. His hands were firm and tanned against the smooth ivory of her skin. He moved the barely-there barrier of her g-string aside with one finger and studied her, intent and intense, his lips parted just enough for Genie to be able to feel the warmth of his breath between her legs.

Genie's heart stopped beating for a few seconds. She'd thought that she'd wanted him to touch her in the lift, but nowhere near as much as she wanted him to put his mouth on her now. And then he did, slow, warm and sure, the sweep of his eyelashes dark on his cheek, his earlier restlessness replaced by unhurried sensuousness; pure gold. Watching him, she smoothed her fingers over his hair, saw each stroke of his tongue a second before the sensation hit her flesh.

The first orgasm Abel had given her had been urgent and extreme, driven by the need for speed. Tonight he took his sweet time, paying attention to her reactions, licking her slowly, circling his tongue harder when it made her fingers grab into his hair to rock herself onto his mouth for more. She lost focus when he laughed, low and sexy, then eased his fingers inside her, drawing her clitoris into his mouth. He had her and he knew it, holding her in his mouth as her muscles jerked and she dug her fingernails into the smooth bulk of his warm, sports-star shoulders.

His breathing was almost as shallow as hers for a few seconds, and he turned his face to drift barely there kisses along her inner thigh before rising to his feet. His cock strained hard against his jeans, but he caught hold of her hand when she reached down to release him.

'Go to bed, Beauty.'

'Come with me?' she asked, quiet, wanting him, wanting to give to him as he'd given to her.

Abel shook his head, and Genie could feel him retreating even though he was as standing as close as he could possibly be.

'That's not how this is gonna go.'

Confusion clouded her mind. She couldn't get the measure of him. He wanted sex with her really, really badly. He might not have said it with words, but his cock couldn't lie.

'How *is* it going to go then, Abel? You get to help yourself to my body but I don't get yours?'

'Don't pretend you didn't like it,' he said. 'You were the one who took your clothes off, lady. I took it that you needed servicing.'

'Needed servicing?' she said, repeating his dumb insult because it took her by surprise so much.

'You heard me right.' He scooped her forwards off the table with his warm hands on her ass and set her down on her feet. 'And now you've *been* serviced, so we can both go and get some sleep.'

Genie hated that the sound that left her lungs sounded like a strangled cat, but it was all she could manage, to articulate the rage and frustration and loathing that formed in her chest as Abel touched his fingers to his brow in mock salute and disappeared into his apartment without glancing back.

Inside his front door, Abel kicked the nearest chair so hard it flew across the room and made for the shower. Again.

Inside her front door, Genie heard the smash. Half of her wanted to go and force him to take what he so obviously needed. The other half of her wanted to smash something herself, preferably something heavy over Abel Kingdom's stupid, beautiful head.

Chapter Nine

The next morning found Genie restless, still wound up and confused as hell. For a man she'd known for barely a week, Abel took up an inordinate amount of her time and her thoughts. She couldn't handle his attitude towards her; the way he made her want him and showed her that he wanted her - then refused to take her. He'd given her two bone-melting orgasms, yet for the most part he seemed like he couldn't stand the sight of her. She wanted to make him come so hard his knees would buckle, yet at the same time she wanted to clamp her hands around his throat and stop his breath. It was exhausting, and she was more than aware that the sexual tension was distracting her from the real and urgent business of raising enough money to keep hold of the theatre. She'd called a meeting with Deanna and the newly recruited Divine Girls later that day. She could only hope that between them they could formulate a plan of action, because left to her own devices, all Genie seemed able to think about was the infuriating man across the hall.

Abel looked up from the plans he'd spread out on the dining table, hearing the knock on the door. Folding them in two, he crossed to open it and found Genie there with a bacon sandwich in her hand.

'I made you breakfast.' She held the plate out and smiled before taking a sip of coffee from the mug in her other hand.

'To say thank you for your orgasm?' he said acidly, even

though it smelled good and he was hungry.

She didn't take the bait, just kept on smiling that pretty girl smile and raised her eyebrows expectantly until he accepted the plate and swept his arm out in resigned invitation. Genie followed him back to the dining table. All traces of last night's showgirl had been erased by her daytime uniform of cut off shorts, tee shirt and tied back hair. She could pass for eighteen, and she sure made him feel like a clueless teenager too. She wrong-footed him at every turn, like this most of all. He didn't know how to be around her when she was this way: unguarded-looking, innocent, and every inch as sexy as her womanly alter ego. More so. Dangerously so, because she brought out his protector gene and made him feel like a prize shit for wanting her theatre.

'Is it good?' she asked, nodding towards the sandwich, sipping her coffee as she perched on a dining chair.

It was good. Really good.

'How old are you, Genie?'

Mild surprise registered in her eyes. 'Twenty-eight. Why?'

He shrugged. 'Nothing. Just… nothing.' He wasn't sure how to articulate it without starting another argument and he preferred his mornings drama-free.

She didn't push him. Maybe she was fresh out of argumentative spirit this morning too. Or maybe she had her own agenda. From the pensive look on her face, he was pretty sure that whatever was on her mind was about to come out of her mouth. He was careful not to let his eyes linger on her lips for long, because every time he did his cock stood up and begged to be fed between them.

'Will you do something for me, Abel?' she said, her voice soft and her gaze direct. He prayed it was something easy, because in that moment he feared there was no way on earth he could say no.

'Go on,' he said, pushing the empty plate away from him and taking a slug of her coffee.

'I just want you to listen to me. A few minutes of your time. No interruptions.'

He had the time. He wasn't certain he wanted to hear what she had to say, but he nodded all the same.

'It's about your opinion of me,' she said, confirming his suspicion that he wasn't going to enjoy the next few minutes.

'Or else your opinion about what I do, which seems to be a problem for you. I'm not sure you understand it, and I want you to. Burlesque isn't cheap, Abel, and it isn't prostitution. It's an age-old form of entertainment, rich in comedy and music hall tradition. It's about striptease, illusion, art… a celebration of women. Yes, it's suggestive. Yes, it's sexy. But it's not obscene, or debasing to the performer or the watchers. When I'm up there on stage, it's… I can't even put it into words how it makes me feel. Powerful, and feminine, and I can feel the audience sharing in that with me. I see it in their eyes, my pleasure amplified in theirs. It's that connection, that appreciation, that makes it so thrilling. So addictive.'

Abel listened to every word and detested them all. Had she finished? Was it his turn to speak now?

'There's something else too. Last night, out there on the landing… that's the first time any man has ever touched me in costume, Abel.'

He reached for her coffee again, needing the scorch to burn away the image of her on that table last night in her tassels and g-string.

The knowledge that no other man had touched her while she was dressed like that did things it shouldn't have done for his ego, perversely making him harsher than he might otherwise have been.

'You done?'

She accepted the mug he pushed back across the table and nodded, her pretty face a mask of subtle hope.

'Nice speech, Beauty. I can see you mean it too. You love your job. You're proud of what you do. I get it. Is that what you want from me?'

Clouds gathered in her eyes. 'Not really, no.'

'Ah.' Abel nodded. 'You want me to agree with you. Well, therein lies the problem, green eyes. You say sexy, I say sexual. The same, but very fucking different. You say music hall tease, I say stripper. You say striptease is a celebration of being a woman. Do you think it feels like that to women who strip in seedy downtown bars for men who want a whole lot more than to appreciate their playful sense of humour?'

Watching her digesting his words, all innocence and ponytails, riled him something chronic. 'Is a high class hooker different to a girl on a street corner, Genie? Just because you work a more classy joint, it doesn't make you any better, darlin'.'

The clouds in her eyes turned full on stormy, telling him he'd hit home. 'That's not fair and you know it, Abel.' She held her body rigid with anger. 'What about what you do? Gyms and whatever. Does that make you representative of those guys who wreck their bodies and their brains with steroids, who flip out and kill their girlfriends in a jealous drug-induced rage? Does that sit heavy on your shoulders?'

Abel huffed. It was completely different. Fitness was a lifestyle choice, not a last resort for people clean out of other options.

'No, I guessed not,' she said, standing up to leave, obviously feeling that she'd won her point. *No. No way.*

He flipped the plans open on the table and her eyes moved over them, widening slowly.

'Why Abel? Why me, why here? Why this personal crusade?'

She didn't have the first fucking clue how personal this was.

'See this?' he said, running his finger over the plans. 'Seven weeks, and then this happens. The precious stage you perform on? Ripped out. The seats your audience ogle you from? Trashed. Gone, the whole fucking lot of it. Too right this is personal, and the reason why is none of your business.'

They were both on their feet, facing each other down across

the table. The fury and hurt in her eyes gratified him and pained him in equal measures.

'Thanks for breakfast. You can leave now,' he said, sarcasm iced through his voice.

'You haven't won yet,' she whispered, hot pink spots burning bright on her cheeks, her fists balled with temper. 'Not by a long chalk, mister. This place is still mine, and I'm not giving it up without a fight.'

'Fine. Have it your own way, but I should warn you… I don't fight fair, lady.'

'Me neither. You haven't seen the half of me.'

He laughed, deliberately mocking her bravado. 'Oh, I think I have, darlin', along with the rest of your *appreciative* audience.'

She was practically shaking. 'I think I actually hate you,' she spat, unguarded in her own fury.

'You should tell that to your body,' he said, shooting her a slow, disdainful look that made her want to gouge his eyes out with her fingernails. 'Only it seemed to disagree with you last night.'

Chapter Ten

Genie glanced from the kitchen towards the five girls assembled in her living room, each of them strikingly different and all of them sexy in their own unique way. She and Deanna had deliberately selected the most seasoned performers from the applications to join The Divine Girls, because time was absolutely of the essence. They needed a show ready to go yesterday, and each of these women came with their acts already highly polished and perfected. Holly and Pearl she already knew quite well from the circuit, both women having performed previously in burlesque showcase nights at the theatre to general acclaim. Holly was as petite as Pearl was tall and as brunette as Pearl was blonde.

Petra was Italian, and dripped Sophia Loren-style sexuality from her exquisitely painted eyes to her heavily accented English. She'd walked into the auditions with nothing more than a copy of an Italian broadsheet newspaper as a prop, and had proceeded to sit on a straight backed chair and disrobe whilst reading the paper in a way that had her all-female audience roundly applauding her skill.

At twenty-one, Delilah was the youngest and least experienced of the girls - not that it was apparent from her act. As all-American as apple pie, she was the sexy cheerleader who actually did what all the guys fantasised the sexy cheerleader would do - stripped off that itty-bitty little uniform *before* she waved her pompoms. Her act was cheeky, the perfect match for her California sunshine personality.

The troupe was completed by Charity, a vintage siren with royal blue pin-curled hair and the smoke-edged voice of an angel, or as close to an angel as an artfully tattooed girl in a spray-on dress can be. It was a toss up which was more mesmerising, her voice or her curves, as she slowly removed her clothes during her performance.

Genie added a milk jug to the coffee tray in Deanna's hands and ushered her friend through to join the others. She reached into the pocket of her jean shorts as she followed behind, pulling out the note Abel had shoved under her door as she'd heard him go out an hour or two earlier. If the way he'd slammed his door and pushed the note so hard under the sill that it had skidded half way across the room was anything to go by, he was still mightily pissed off. *Good.* She wanted him wound up and not thinking straight. She wanted him goddamn furious. Maybe it'd force a little honesty out of him. And deep down dark and hidden, she just plain wanted him, which made her furious with herself most of all, because however unreasonable, the urge was as unstoppable as breathing. Her head was a mess of hating everything he stood for and at the same instant wanting his hands everywhere on her.

Deanna was speaking to the girls, assuming her natural role as campaign leader and organiser-in-chief. The gathered women gasped in shock at the news of the grave threat to the theatre, and Genie was buoyed by their sympathy and the way they banded together and threw themselves unanimously behind the plan to help raise funds.

Within a couple of hours they'd organised an intensive rehearsal and performance schedule and Deanna had taken charge of admin and marketing to get the people through the door.

Times like these, Genie was very glad to be a woman: she couldn't imagine a group of men ever bonding together without their competitive spirits forcing them to try to assert themselves over each other first. Amen to sisterhood.

As the group quietened, Genie smoothed out the note from Abel and laid it on the coffee table in the midst of the group.

'Kingdom sent me this today. He's bringing a group of investors to look around the building on Friday afternoon and wants me to make myself scarce.'

Deanna half laughed, half snorted. 'He's got some nerve.'

'Maybe these investors can be persuaded to invest in you instead,' Pearl speculated, her blue eyes sparkling with trouble.

Holly laughed, clapping her hands. 'Ladies, we need to be downstairs on Friday afternoon. All of us, yes?' Her eyes slid around the other girls' answering grins, all of them on the let's-screw-over-Abel-Kingdom wavelength.

'We're gonna scorch their fuckin' eyeballs out,' Delilah's laugh was pure filth.

Petra folded her legs beneath her on the couch, cat-like. 'I shall read them the business supplement from my newspaper.' Her deep, throaty voice turned everything she said into an accented, X-rated purr.

'So what's he like, this Abel guy?' Holly asked, her head tipped to one side. 'Is he hot?'

Genie's eyes slid to Deanna's, who shrugged and held her hands up in the air. 'I'll leave that one to you to answer,' her friend said, and all eyes in the room turned to Genie.

'No,' Genie started vehemently, and then hesitated. 'Well, kind of.' She rallied. 'But not once you get to know him.'

'He's blistering,' Deanna supplied helpfully, and rolled her eyes when Genie shot her daggers. 'Well he is,' she said. 'Not that it matters, but he is. In fact, you girls need to know that now so you can steel yourselves against him. He might try to divide and conquer.'

Genie nodded, mute, thinking of him dividing her legs and conquering her on the hallway table the night before. She pulled herself up out of the armchair as the girls gathered up their belongings, and hugged each of them in turn before she reached for the catch on the front door.

'Thank you, guys,' she said. ' I really mean it. This place is everything to me.'

She swung the door wide and stepped into the hallway, realising a beat too late that she could hear footsteps on the stairs.

There was only ever one person that it was going to be, and as the girls filed out from behind her onto the landing, Abel appeared at the top of the steps. He stood stock still for a second, clearly taken aback by the unexpected sight of the six women lined up in front of him. Genie noticed the subtle shift in the energy amongst the group, from camaraderie to speculation. The flare of a bent knee, the tipped up hip. The invitation of a subtly raised eyebrow. The folded arms to draw attention to high breasts. Every last girl offered Abel something new to look at, and it took Genie a few seconds to process the common expression in all of their eyes.

Not invitation. *Challenge*. They weren't offering themselves to Abel Kingdom. They were throwing down the gauntlet. *Take us on if you dare*. Genie looked down at the floor for a second to hide her grin, and wanted to hug each of the newly formed Divine Girls all over again for their show of unity.

Petra broke ranks first, stepping forward and extending her hand delicately towards Abel. 'Arrivederci, Mr Kingdom,' she practically growled, holding his hand for a few seconds too long before brushing past him and heading downstairs.

Holly stepped up next, laying her hand on Abel's forearm. 'I've heard so much about you, Mr Kingdom,' she murmured, batting her lashes as she skipped off down the stairs after Petra.

'All of it bad,' Pearl added, laughing lightly, moving forward and brushing her lips against Abel's cheek as she stepped past him. Abel touched his fingers against his cheek, frowning as his eyes met Genie's big innocent ones.

Charity followed Pearl, her blue waves arranged over one shoulder as she stepped in front of Abel and touched her lips against his other cheek. 'Until next time, Mr Kingdom,' she murmured as she moved away towards the stairs.

Delilah's Californian smile wreathed her face as she followed the rest of the girls' lead and approached Abel. 'You're every bit as hot as I'd imagined,' she said, running an appreciate hand over Abel's bicep as she moved around him to the staircase. She said it straight, but the mockery in her intention was clear enough. Genie wanted to laugh. Priceless. Well played, ladies.

Deanna was last to move forward, placing her palm flat against Abel's chest as she leaned forward. 'She says hot, I say dickhead,' she whispered against his neck, too quietly for Genie to catch her words. 'Fuck with my friend and you fuck with us all, sunshine.'

And then there was just Genie and Abel on the landing, eying each other speculatively.

'Another pyjama party, green eyes?' he said, his keys jangling in his hand.

'Wouldn't you love to know,' Genie muttered, shoving her hands in the back pockets of her shorts to ensure they didn't reach out of their own accord and touch him.

'No need. It's all in here already thanks to your pretty friends,' he tapped his finger against his forehead. 'Us guys are all about the visuals. But then you don't need me to tell *you* what turns men on, do you?'

Genie caught his implied slur and batted it right back with an exaggerated sigh. 'Change the record Abel. You're starting to bore me.'

He laughed softly as he opened his front door. 'There aren't going to be any changes to my plan, Genie. You and the Kids from Fame go ahead and give it your best shot.' He stepped inside and turned back to look at Genie, tossing his keys up and catching them deftly in mid air. 'I'll be waiting right here at the end of it all to take the keys to this whole building from your uncle, not just this apartment.'

He clicked his door closed behind him, leaving Genie standing alone in the hall with just fury and frustration for company.

Friday lunchtime found The Divine Girls gathered once more in the theatre, but this time downstairs rather than in Genie's apartment. The foyer, so often thronged with excited theatregoers, was thronged today with a clientele of a different kind. Almost exclusively women, a palpable sizzle of excitement in the air, an undertone of camaraderie and feminine sensuality.

Deanna had made sure to spread the word far and wide about the event, an afternoon of free burlesque instruction with The Divine Girls. The invitation had suggested attendees dress for an afternoon of frolics and burlesque fun, and they'd also provided an impromptu lending wardrobe for those who didn't own anything suitable.

Genie was on the stage, Charity held court in the bar, turning it into a sultry saloon bar of bygone days. Deanna worked the kiosk, transformed for the afternoon into the sexiest of usherettes. Petra had set up camp in the auditorium, an innocent looking pile of newspapers and a line of straight-backed chairs her only props. Delilah was in command of the foyer, the heavy drapes drawn across the theatre doors to preserve their privacy from the street.

Holly and Pearl had teamed up for the afternoon to offer instruction in the art of posing, teasing, glove peeling and even tassel twirling for those brave enough to try it, whilst Genie held fan classes on the stage. In short, they were teaching women how to seduce, giving them a peek into the old-fashioned art of burlesque.

Deanna's double whammy marketing ploy meant firstly that the women would hopefully return home full of excitement about the spectacle and book tickets to bring their friends and lovers back to see the new Divine Girls show. Equally importantly, the gathering would have the effect of utterly derailing Abel's meeting with his bunch of straight-laced investors. He wanted to show a bunch of suits around? Sure. Let him try. They'd make sure that they saw the real, living theatre at its very best.

Genie glanced at the clock at the back of the auditorium. He was due at one, and it was quarter to. Any time now then. Nerves swirled low in her stomach, both because she needed to pull this off and because she knew Abel was going to be more furious than ever with her. It was his own damn fault, with his selective prejudices and his pigheaded stubbornness.

Charity's smoky voice drifted through from the bar, setting the tone for the whole event, accompanied today by Deanna's cocktail connoisseur brother who manned the bar, lubricating proceedings with free Cosmopolitans to help loosen inhibitions and basque strings.

Genie's first fan class had just ended, and she took five minutes to walk through the theatre for one final check. It was all going swimmingly. Holly had her audience of ten enthralled, each of them mimicking her actions as she demonstrated how to remove her long satin gloves, tugging delicately at each fingertip with her teeth before peeling it off with a flourish. Pearl moved amongst the class, murmuring encouragements and tips to the women as they practised. 'Hold eye contact, that's right. Now sway your hips a little. Use your whole body, not just your hands.' Genie heard her say. 'It's all about confidence. You're all beautiful women, now sashay!'

Genie couldn't have said it better herself, and she needed to hear it too just then. In the auditorium she observed Petra's class in full flow, every chair now occupied by a sexily dressed woman learning the arts of Sunday morning newspaper seduction.

Delilah was the welcoming committee nearest to the front doors, her masterclass in very adult cheerleading a roaring success. She'd already taught the group several chants in readiness for Abel's arrival, which was timely, because as Genie moved into the kiosk beside Deanna, the small window onto the street allowed her to glimpse him approaching from across the street with several associates in tow.

It was the first time she'd seen him in business dress, and for a few seconds he knocked her breathless. He was a powerful man, and the dark grey, well-fitted suit served only to enhance that, lending him an extra air of authority that filled her with apprehension. He wasn't her cocky Australian neighbour right now. He was a world class businessman who she was about to royally screw over.

It wasn't that she felt bad for doing it, it was more that she was suddenly terrified of his reaction. She was under no illusions about how formidable an adversary he was and she knew there would be retaliation of some kind.

Deanna's hand snaked into hers beneath the counter and squeezed it. 'Game on,' she murmured, catching Genie's eye with a mischievous grin. Genie swallowed hard and nodded as she watched Abel approach the glass theatre doors, noting the way his step slowed a little as he clocked the closed curtains, his first indication that all was not as he'd expected in the theatre. She saw his brows lower into a frown as he reached forwards and pushed the door open.

On cue, Delilah's crew of cheerleaders swung into action, shaking their pompoms and chanting out the letters of Abel's surname as they shimmied. K. I. N. G. D. O. M! Who's the sexiest of them all? Kingdom!

Genie watched, torn between looking at the dancing girls, at Abel's clearly agog associates, and at Abel himself. He won. She saw the thunder pass over his face as he listened to the chant, and then the way he regrouped within moments and rewarded the girls with a killer smile as they finished with a shimmy and a shake. Delilah turned a graceful cartwheel, coming to a halt in front of Abel's investors.

'Welcome to Theatre Divine, gentlemen,' she said, her all-American cheerleader's confidence leaving them no choice but to accept the hand she offered to each of them in turn. Genie watched her in action and thanked her lucky stars and stripes that the Californian girl was here, stripping these guys of their professional intentions before they'd taken more than ten steps inside the building. And they were all guys, not a woman among them. Genie might in other circumstances have considered this a sorry state of affairs, but today it suited her purposes entirely; she had in fact banked on the imbalance.

Abel caught sight of Genie as she moved from behind the kiosk and crossed the space between them. The cordial smile didn't leave his face, but she didn't miss the fire in his dark eyes.

'That's some welcoming committee, huh guys?' he laughed easily for the benefit of the men behind him, although he'd kind of lost his audience. Leaning in as if to deliver a cordial kiss on Genie's cheek, he took the opportunity instead to speak, his voice soft and deadly in her ear. 'You'll fucking pay for this, green eyes.' He pulled back as if he hadn't spoken, seeming to everyone else in the foyer still the smiling guy in charge.

Or battling to stay in charge, as it was swiftly turning into a fight for the investors' attention. Deanna walked around the kiosk in sky high heels, her itsy-bitsy cherry pink usherette suit moulded to her curves as she carried a tray of Manhattans with the ease of a girl trained ruthlessly by her bartender brother in her student years.

'Cocktail, sir?' she asked the guy closest to her, a sandy haired exec who'd already shed his jacket and loosened his tie. He tried and failed to keep his eyes from Deanna's cleavage as he helped himself from the proffered tray. His associates followed suit without a second thought, leaving Abel the only man without a glass in his hand.

Delilah had picked off the guy closest to her, her blonde ponytail swinging as she invented a chant on the spot made up of his name. She had him mesmerised. Whatever he'd come here for today had clearly gone out of his head entirely as he basked under the glow of Delilah's attention. Genie smiled down at the floor, her fingers crossed behind her back. One down. Several more to go. Abel cleared his throat.

'Shall we, gentlemen?' he said. 'This way.'

The group followed his lead with varying degrees of

reluctance, leaving behind the guy Delilah had enchanted with her transatlantic smile and tanned limbs.

Abel headed for the back of the foyer, knowing there was a door there to lead his group into the non- public areas of the building. Genie knew it too of course, and had locked it earlier that day. She saw him try the handle twice and then turn to look towards her with murder in his eyes. She shrugged, feigning surprise at the fact that his way was once more blocked.

Petra chose the moment he led his group back into the auditorium to rise from her chair and call her class to order, ten women lined up on high backed chairs in front of her. She didn't bother to glance towards Abel or his group, but they were a stone's throw from where she worked and she knew it full well.

'Okay girls,' Petra purred, winding her body around the chair as she spoke. 'It's Sunday morning. You're at home, in your kitchen. Your husband wants bacon. You want sex. This is what you do. Watch me first, and then you will learn.' Her exotically accented voice was none the less clear and rang out as she sat down, crossed her elegant legs, picked up the newspaper and flicked it open. Every man in the room turned to watch her at the mention of the word sex, as instinctive as Pavlov's dogs. Even Abel reacted without thinking before he got himself in check, turning determinedly away from watching the beautiful raven haired woman as she began her act.

Genie glanced at his group, which now resembled a party of her theatregoers rather than a bunch of Abel's high-powered business colleagues, their ties loosened, shirt sleeves pushed back, glasses in their hands, refreshed by Deanna with a knowing smile. Realising that he'd once more lost his audience, Abel left them raptly watching Petra and stalked over to Genie beside the kiosk.

'What the hell is this?' he said, his anger barely concealed. 'Your idea of a fucking ambush?'

'It's hardly an ambush,' Genie laughed softly, revelling in his annoyance and her clear mastery of the situation. Beyond where they stood, Petra had removed most of her outfit and had Abel's guys visibly gagging for her to lower that newspaper.

'Candy from a baby, Abel.' She murmured, but as she went to walk away she caught her breath when his fingers closed around her wrist.

'You really think you can stop me?' he breathed, his eyes hot on hers. Looking into them, Genie wasn't sure of anything at all.

'Let go of me. I've a class to teach.'

He all but hissed. 'You're not performing for these guys. No fucking way.'

'Since when did you get to tell me what I can and can't do?' she said coolly, both thrilled and appalled by his territorial words. 'And I'm not performing for them. I'm performing for the women in my class. If your investors happen to want to watch too…' she shrugged her shoulders and shook her wrist free of his fingers. Behind her Deanna discreetly distributed the information packs she'd put together, outlining their plans to save and preserve Theatre Divine as a burlesque hotspot. Genie saw the men file them with their other paperwork and her heart banged against her ribs with hope.

'Seems like Petra's show's over,' she said. 'You might want to go and try to get your audience back.'

She turned and walked through into the auditorium, privately doubting he'd be able to recover the attention of his business associates. They were already heading in the same direction that she was, no doubt enticed by the sounds coming from Holly and Pearl's masterclass in progress. Abel followed them reluctantly. The two performers worked together to demonstrate their skills to their watchful students, Holly commentating as Pearl exhibited her signature technique of unlacing the back of a corset whilst throwing a wink over her shoulder towards anyone who should be watching. Her hips moved in time with the sensual sound of Charity's voice in the bar, her deft fingers unravelling the ribbons criss-crossing her back, with slow, precise flourishes.

Abel halted and crossed his arms over his chest, no doubt

more than aware that he didn't stand a chance of trying to make those guys listen to dry business propositions when they were surrounded by an array of beautiful women taking their clothes off.

'You said it yourself, Abel.' Genie leaned towards him as if confiding in him. 'Men are visual creatures.'

She left him standing there on the edge of the group, knowing from his lethal expression that he wanted to lynch her, though he had no choice but to let her walk away.

Abel watched Genie walk towards the stage, his fists balled at his sides to prevent him from ripping the nearest seat clean out of the floor in fury. She'd taken his words and turned them on him, and the worst of it was that she was patently right. His carefully gathered group of investors had become more akin to a bunch of men on a Saturday night stag do, and they could scarcely be held accountable, given the wall to wall provocation that Genie and co had presented them with.

He'd known she had fire in her belly, but he hadn't counted on her being so goddamn creative and tenacious. In other circumstances he'd admire her guts, maybe, but not today. She had mustered her resourcefulness only to throw obstacles in his path. And that's all they are, he reminded himself. Obstacles. He'd climbed over bigger, tougher obstacles in his life than this woman could ever hope to put in his way. He'd get what he wanted in the end.

And then the spotlight illuminated the stage, and all he wanted in that moment was the girl perched atop the glittering lamp that rose from the stage. *How did she do that?* She was the last woman on earth he wanted to want, yet she bleached out all traces of his common sense with a flick of her eyes and the slide of her hands down her own body. Almost everyone in the place, men and women alike, gravitated towards the stage to occupy the front rows of the theatre stalls and listen to Genie's master class.

Abel leaned against a nearby pillar, wanting to walk away, knowing full well that he wouldn't. She'd transformed again, no longer the girl or the businesswoman, once more the seductress. She reminded him of iconic film stars of yesteryear, all curves and confidence.

Everyone listened as she spoke about the various props she used in her acts and regaled them with tales of burlesque stars and their signature moves over the ages. She was a natural performer, speaking as well as dancing, her audience listened raptly as she offered advice on more everyday props that they could try out easily at home.

A woman in the front row raised her hand as Genie's talk came to an end amidst lengthy applause and even a few whoops of appreciation.

'Do you think we could see your act with the lamp?'

An excited murmur of assent rippled through the small crowd.

'She's amazing,' Holly grinned and dropped into a seat amongst the gathered spectators. 'Just wait until you see this.'

Genie's eyes scanned the assembled faces quickly and Abel thought he could read apprehension in her body language for the briefest of seconds before she shrugged prettily. 'Of course. It won't be quite the same without the orchestra or the lighting techs, but it'll give you the idea of how I get the most out of the lamp as a prop.'

In the wings, Deanna was ready to go with Genie's practice soundtrack, and Abel slunk lower into his chair at the back of the auditorium as the now familiar slide of the trumpets heralded the start of Genie's routine. He knew pretty much move for move what she was going to do up there, but in this case knowledge wasn't power. Watching Genie rendered him powerless. Powerless to take his eyes off her. Powerless to stop his body reacting to hers. Powerless to stop the bewildering mix of lust and contempt low in his gut, whether contempt for her or for himself, he wasn't sure. She stirred memories in him he'd rather keep buried, and she stirred emotions in him that left him feeling betrayed even by his own body. Right at that moment his head hated her, his cock loved her, and his heart was plain confused.

The would-be investors watched with open admiration as Genie performed for the group, her act rendered all the more intimate by the unusually small audience. *What if it were smaller still? What would it be like to be the only observer, to have her perform just for him?* The thought disquieted Abel, sending his hand scrubbing harshly over the dark stubble on his clenched jaw. He'd never allow himself to be in that position, so it didn't matter.

Up on the stage Genie's fingers picked apart the ribbons holding her corset in place, and Abel steeled himself. He was going to see a hell of a lot of peaches and cream skin in around five seconds, and he needed to school himself not to want to punch the lights out of every other man in the room for seeing and appreciating that exact same sight.

He'd got things badly wrong today. He'd woefully underestimated the almost naked woman up there on the stage, and God knows why, because he was fighting a daily battle to stay both ahead of her and away from her. She had too many faces. An angel in cut off shorts and innocent plaits, an unexpectedly shrewd and calculating opponent in business. But coated in glitter and very little else, surveying her kingdom from the top of that goddamn lamp, she was nothing less than demonic.

Abel slipped out of the stage door of the theatre just after eleven that night, his hand shoved deep into the pockets of his jeans and his dark head down. He didn't need to look up at the street names to find his way, or check his phone for a map of the area.

He knew the way. He knew these streets. They were etched on him, all over him, like newsprint that wouldn't scrub off. He'd been a child here, a teenager, a punchbag every now and then.

Too young back then to have control over his circumstances, those years had discoloured big chunks of his soul black. There had been no light and shade to his childhood, and right here right now, he needed to stamp all over those memories, stamp hard until they were ground into the pavement beneath his boots.

London rain hung damp in the air, cool on his face as his steps slowed by the still familiar school gates. Painted smartly in red now instead of peeling blue, but still there, still the same. Most kids had hated this place. Not Abel. School had been his respite, his safe place, his guaranteed square meal of the day. Not that he'd had many friends; his mother wasn't exactly the type to let him bring anyone home to tea. She was more likely to have their fathers round after hours.

He'd been the kind of child who flew just under the radar; his running shoes never cool enough, scraping in at the last minute with his homework so the teachers didn't single him out. It had eroded him more than even he realised, worn him down into a survival pattern made up mostly of keeping his eyes down and his mouth shut. It was a lonely way, but an effective one. He'd been a ghost amongst them, getting by, biding his time.

Just being back on these familiar streets sent a shiver of distaste down his back, more unpalatable than the drizzle on his face. He'd worked hard to shake off the dirt those years had coated him in, and being here again he could feel it trying to reattach itself, layer by subtle layer. Walking these pavements again now, sub-consciously avoiding the lines just as he had as a kid. If I don't stand on the cracks she'll be out when I get home. If I don't stand on the cracks she might be home alone. If I don't stand on the cracks she might love me some more.

It was an ordinary house in a run down back street, a shabby two-up two-down mid terrace with paper-thin walls and no garden. Sitting on the wall of the boarded up house opposite, Abel stared at it. He'd kept a loose track of her over the years, knew it was still the place she called home, even if he didn't. Was she in there right now? The flickering, blueish light cast from the

TV in the uncurtained downstairs front room would suggest so.

He zipped his jacket close against his body, colder than the weather dictated he ought to be. A shadow moved across the room, his mother, surely, halting, looking, and then the room fell into darkness. Was she standing in the window watching him? Had she recognised him? Would she come outside any second now? Abel could hear his heartbeat loud inside his head as he stared at the front door, half ready to run if it opened. In that moment, he wasn't a successful businessman in control of his own life. He was her son again, small and skinny, scared and desperate for her approval. Clammy-handed, he held his breath, letting it go again when a lamp fleetingly illuminated the upstairs window before falling dark again. She hadn't seen him after all. Just as he'd done as a child, he moved quietly away, staying in the shadows, hot relief pumping through his veins at not having had to face her.

Chapter Eleven

'That was some stunt you pulled yesterday,' Abel said, sauntering towards the stage with a notebook in his hand.

Genie stopped running her hands over the lamp to check for damage and turned to look down at him.

'If nothing else, I hope it made you realise how serious I am about keeping this place.'

Abel made a point of noting something down and then looked back up. 'Six weeks and six days,' he stated baldly.

He dropped down into a central seat on the front row, his long legs thrown in front of him, his notebook discarded on the seat next to him so he could fold his arms across his chest. He looked like a guy watching a game, lounging around in battered jeans and an old tee shirt, totally at ease, even though Genie was sure he had to be anything but. She had seen enough of him to know that the last place he liked to be was anywhere near her work.

'Have you come for a private show?' she asked, unable to resist goading him, even though she was perfectly well aware that it was the last thing he wanted.

'I've seen everything you've got to offer, Beauty.' He shook his head and laughed low, but he didn't fool her. She didn't miss the flicker in his eyes, kind of hunted, kind of hunter.

'You think so?' she asked, looking for his weakness. He had to have one. Everyone did, and she needed to find his fast if she was going to work out how to beat him. There was blatant sexual chemistry between them, and it certainly wasn't that that he was afraid of. She had no doubt that he'd be a confident, accomplished lover. On the occasions he'd let her near, he'd shown her that he was perfectly capable of melting her bones if he wanted to. Not that she wanted him to right here and now, of course. Definitely not. But there was something complicated going on just beneath the surface, a button she sensed she could press if she could just work out where the hell it was.

She wanted to stay in control here, to press home her advantage after the triumph of the investor visit. Fleetingly wishing she'd dressed in something a little less revealing than her cut off jean shorts, albeit topped with a sweatshirt, she hopped up to sit on top of the lamp. The added height of her new vantage point did a couple of things: it placed her in a position of superiority over him, and it brought that look straight back into his eyes again. *Interesting.* What was it for him? Was it that he didn't like not being in charge? Maybe she was dressed right for this encounter after all.

'Seeing as you're here, maybe you can help me out,' she said casually. Her opening salvo. 'I've been thinking of changing my routine a little.'

She stretched her bare legs out along the length of the lamp, letting her body follow the curves of the prop. 'At the moment, I do this…' She leaned backwards, lying down, unclipping her hair as she went back so that it fell down the side of the lamp. 'And then this…' she ran her hands over her body, and then sighed loudly with dissatisfaction. 'Hang on.' She sat up and reached for the hem of her top. 'I can't do it in this sweatshirt.'

'Genie, quit fuckin…'

Too slow. Genie peeled the sweat top over her head and then shook her hair out, drawing pleasure from the fact that he didn't look as cocky any more.

'That's better,' she said, resuming her position, running her hands over her body again. 'I do this, and then I… oh, hell.' She sat up again. 'I really need to lose the vest to show you what I mean.'

'Do not, NOT take any more goddamn clothes off, Genie. I'm warning you.' His voice was low and lethal.

She paused.

'You're warning me?'

He stared her down, not moving an inch, but the way his fingers gripped his own biceps hard enough to bruise betrayed him.

'I don't take kindly to being threatened, Abel,' she said softly. 'Especially not in my own home.'

She didn't, but she was also one hundred percent certain that Abel's warning wasn't an aggressive one. Not physically. He was many things, but Genie knew in her gut that this wasn't a man who'd ever hurt a woman with his hands. His words, sure, she knew that already, and his actions, but never his fists. Maybe that was why she felt defiant enough to disregard his threat and haul her vest up, swirling it on one fingertip before letting it fall onto the stage below her.

Abel watched her, his silence practically yelling at her that she was pushing him too far.

'That's better,' she smiled, sliding her hands up over her now naked rib cage. 'You'll just have to imagine I'm wearing nipple tassels. Would it help if I took my bra off?' She reached behind her, and he was out of his seat and up on the stage in less than two seconds. One fluid movement later, she found herself hauled off the lamp and thrown over his shoulder as if he were rescuing her from a burning building.

She'd tried to push his buttons, and it appeared that she'd succeeded. His warm forearm clamped rock solid against the back of her thighs as he strode down the steps at the side of the stage back onto the auditorium floor. He pulled her roughly down his body, and she caught him unawares and snagged her legs around his waist. She wasn't done with him yet.

'Too much for you, Popeye?'

Her ass was in his hands, and his chest heaved beneath hers.

'What the fuck are you trying to prove?' he said, more serious than she'd expected.

She shrugged, her hands on his shoulders.

'That you don't understand what I do?'

He laughed, a harsh, unfunny sound. 'I know what you do. You take your clothes off for money.'

Genie slid her hands into the dark hair at the back of his neck. Silk.

'Aren't you the lucky one. You just got it for free.'

He was mad as hell with her. The tautness of his body told her so. The grip of his hands told her so. But he was turned on too. The demanding heat in his eyes told her so, the fact that he held her clamped against him rather than pushing her away told her so.

'I don't want what you have to give, showgirl. Free or otherwise.'

Showgirl. That was his button. Genie moved her hips, and his hands massaged her ass in a way that contradicted every last one of his words. He wanted it, and she wanted him to admit it. Not because it would change his mind about taking the theatre, but because it would change his mind about her. It shouldn't matter what he thought of her, but there in that moment, it really, really did.

'I'm not just a showgirl, Abel,' she murmured. 'I'm a woman.'

He dropped his eyes to her pale breasts encased in nude coloured lace.

'I see that.'

'Do you?' she whispered. 'Do you really, Abel?'

He shifted her in his arms, holding her easily, one arm under her ass, his other hand sliding up her back. She'd been close against him before, but now he pressed her slowly closer, vertebra by vertebra. He stopped when he reached her bra strap. Her arms were around his neck, and his mouth hovered breath-close to hers.

'You're playing a dangerous game, Genie.' He brushed his

mouth against hers, tasting her, brief and hot and not enough as his fingers opened the catch of her bra and splayed flat on her naked back.

'You don't take your clothes off. I take them off you.'

He peeled her bra from her body as he backed up and rested his ass on the edge of the stage. He jostled her over his crotch, strained denim against denim.

'Play my dangerous game with me?' she breathed, turned on now, losing her grip on her original agenda for the encounter, moving against him, watching his eyes darken to black and demanding.

She closed her eyes when he touched her breasts, firm palms, assured fingers, his mouth on hers as her nipples hardened for him.

'Like this, Beauty?' he said, turning around to sit her on the stage, her legs still wrapped around him. He dipped his head and kissed her breasts, holding them in his hands, licking hotly over her nipples. She watched his mouth, her fingers in his hair, her breath in short supply when he raised his eyes to hers.

'Play games, huh? You want me to play with your tits, like this?' His tongue circled her nipple and he closed his eyes for a second, as if he couldn't help it, as if the pleasure of the moment demanded it. Watching him lick her and lose himself in her body was an aphrodisiac more heady than the most expensive champagne.

'Yes,' she said, barely audible, but he must have caught it anyway, because he opened his dark eyes slowly and she saw the acknowledgment there. Somewhere along the line he'd taken back the power; somewhere in the possessive way he held her, in the way he dictated the pace now as his mouth drifted up her neck. Genie wrapped herself around him, loving the strength of him, the breadth of him between her thighs. He was hard, and hot, and he'd gone straight to her head. If this was his idea of a game, she was ready to play her hand.

'My turn. You want me to play with your cock, Abel?' she

said, covering him with her hand, between their bodies. The thought of touching him like this turned her on as much as being touched by him. He groaned, jerked a little, his tongue moving in her mouth as she unbuttoned his jeans and his resolve. And then she had his cock in her hand, naked and hard for her, his hips rocking against her crotch in a way that told her how far down the line he already was.

She wound her fingers around the thickness of his shaft, her other hand pushed into the hair at the back of his head, holding his mouth to hers as he finally let her give him what he craved. His kiss went from skilled and controlled to ragged breathing into her mouth, his tongue restlessly moving, and she let her tongue slide over his as he sank his teeth into her lower lip and thrust himself steadily into the curve of her fingers. He was lost, eyes screwed shut, his forehead against hers, his hand possessive over her breast.

'Beauty,' he breathed, his voice fractured in his throat. 'Beauty.'

It was the only word he had, and the only one she wanted to hear as she wrapped him in closer with her legs and followed his accelerating rhythm stroke for stroke, holding him firm until he clamped her hard against him and gasped, harsh and animal, his cock jerking rigid in her hand. She held him, wide-eyed and breathless, overtaken by mixed up feelings of pride and lust and protectiveness. She'd done it. She'd pushed him to a place where he'd lost control, and as his breathing steadied and his body settled, she found she wanted only to do it over and over again.

Abel kissed her neck, slow and open mouthed as his heartbeat slid down towards where it needed to be to survive. She tasted sexy, of warm vanilla and turned on woman. Her nipple stiffened under the lazy slide of his thumb, and the moan she made when he let his fingers drift down to rest on her inner thigh had him half way towards hard again, which was fucking ridiculous.

Her shorts were indecent, and he was glad of it.

'Your move,' she said against his ear, daring him on.

He slid his tongue into her mouth again and his fingers under the frayed denim.

'You sure you still want to play games, Beauty?' he whispered, pushing the wisp of her underwear to the side and running the back of his fingers over her. 'You want me to play with you like this?' He pushed a finger between her lips, opening her, pausing. 'Yes?'

She opened her eyes, still kissing him, telling him yes with her eyes and her warm, wanting body. He let his fingers hover, brush her, skim where she needed him most. Deep rose spots tinged her usually pale cheeks, and a damp tendril of hair clung to her face. She looked like a woman on the edge of something amazing, and that he was going to be the one to give her that something amazing tapped into a place so base, so primal, somewhere he'd never been before. It was sex on a whole different level. Jesus, he wanted to fuck this woman just about more than he'd wanted anything in his whole life.

He unfurled his fingers inside her shorts, cupping her, delicately circling her clit with his index finger, making her moan and sink her teeth into his shoulder. Her fingers sought his cock again, and she was gasping, so close. He could be inside her in three seconds. He needed to be inside her in one. He pushed her back until she rested on her elbows, her body bared and begging for him, and then he opened his eyes and all he could see was that huge fucking golden lamp. She was right there, open and wanting him, and all he could think of was how she looked draped over that goddamn thing performing for other men night after night.

What the fuck was he doing? This wasn't okay. This was every kind of wrong. Pulling his hand from her shorts, he pushed himself backwards and away from her, dragging his jeans up and wiping the back of his hand over his mouth.

Genie struggled back to sitting, frustrated shock and

confusion all over her beautiful face. Mad as he was, he still had to fight down the urge to drag her back into his arms, to fill his hands with her creamy curves and think to hell with it. But he couldn't. Not here, with that huge fuck off lamp dominating his eye line, reminding him who she was, what she represented.

'What's wrong?' she said, the look of lust falling fast from her face.

Abel finished buttoning his jeans. 'You got what you wanted there, eh Beauty? You wanted to prove to me that you could get me going, and you have. Good for you.'

She slid off the stage, still naked aside from her cut-offs.

'Why do you do that?' she said, anger rattling in her voice. 'What the fuck is your problem, Abel?'

He really wished she'd put some clothes on.

'Don't mistake me for someone who you can wind around your little finger with sex, Genie,' he warned. 'You're a woman, I'm a man. You want to tempt me into fucking you? Go ahead. Throw yourself at me, it'll be my pleasure. But know this. I'll fuck you, and then I'll fuck you over. You won't stop me taking this theatre by flashing your tits and opening your legs.'

Her sharp intake of breath told him that his words had hurt. A flush of heat raced over her neck and down over the curves of her naked breasts. He battled to keep his eyes on hers rather than on her body.

'That wasn't what happened there and you damn well know it,' she said, covering her breasts with her hands. It didn't help. It just made him want to cover her breasts with *his* hands instead. Fucking, fucking woman with her delicious curves and her fragility and her head full of theatrical dreams, she was pushing him beyond his limits.

'From where I'm standing that's pretty much exactly what happened,' he said, carefully controlled. 'You took your clothes off and threw yourself at me again. It's getting pretty boring, Beauty.'

He'd told some lies in his life but that was up there with the best of them. She didn't bore him. She electrified him.

'You didn't seem bored when I had your cock in my hands ten minutes ago,' she shot back, and he admired her all the more for coming out fighting.

'I'm a man, Genie. We're simple creatures. You touch our cocks, we get stupid. It's chemical. Then you stop touching our cocks and our brains function again and we go about our business as usual, which in my case happens to mean buying this theatre.' He paused and raised an eyebrow at her. 'So unless you plan to spend the next few weeks in bed with me around the clock, you're going to need a better plan.'

'You really think you're something special, don't you?' she said, shaking her head.

'You seemed to think so too back there.'

She laughed and shook her head. 'Dream on. I'm a woman. We don't get stupid when you touch us. We think about a million and one things at the same time. The shopping list. Buying a new couch. Stuff. You get the picture.'

It was his turn to laugh, shoving his hands into his pockets as he made for the door. 'Liar. The only thing on your mind when I was touching you was how fucking good I made you feel.'

'Except you didn't, did you? You conveniently made sure you got your own rocks off and then left me half way goddamn there,' she shouted, full of temper, and a second later she hurled his notebook at his back. 'Here, you forgot this.' His pen followed the book through the air.

'Abel Kingdom is a selfish fuckwit when it comes to sex.' Write *that* down in your fucking notebook.'

Genie pulled on her clothes and sat for a while on the stage after he'd gone, her back resting against the lamp, drawing idle patterns in the left over glitter on the stage. She'd kind of thought that flirting with him on stage would help her to understand his hang-ups, but it had worked against her completely. All it had proved was that his rivers ran too deep and too fast, and that he was capable of seducing her with a look from ten paces away. The raw sexuality of him overwhelmed her. She couldn't fathom him, and she needed to or he was going to take everything she loved away from her.

She knew also that her parting shot had been unfair. In their encounters to date, she was definitely one up when it came to taking rather than giving.

Looking down, realising that she'd absently written his name in glitter, she scrubbed it out in temper.

Abel sat on the back staircase with his head in his hands. Fuck, fuck, fuck. Genie Divine was turning his world upside down. She was the poster girl for just about everything in life that made his skin crawl, and the fact that he couldn't stop himself from wanting her despite that fact made him hate his own reflection in the mirror in the mornings.

What kind of a man was he? He didn't fuck strippers. He didn't pay women to turn him on. He refused to align himself with the strippers he'd known and the men who'd paid them. He'd worked too hard to build a simple, clean life for himself to be dragged back into all of that now.

Rationally, he could see that what Genie did was different from the career his mother had been forced into. Or carved out for herself. As a boy he'd felt sure that she had little alternative but to make a living from her body, yet when he'd offered her a way out as a grown man she'd refused his help. It had been a hard truth to face that his mother was content with her lifestyle, that she'd chosen it over a new start in Australia with him. She had always chosen her lifestyle over anything he meant or could offer her.

He'd made decent money, expecting to rescue her, breeze in and take her away from the grit and grime and sordidness. Absence really had made the heart grow fonder, only it had been one-sided. He'd been prepared to forgive the years of instability and fear, had fooled himself that she lived a life feeling guilty for everything he'd endured, had perhaps only done it in some misguided or desperate attempt to provide for him.

Knowing for sure that she didn't need rescuing hurt, and knowing that she didn't care about reconciling with him hurt more. But his unhappiness as a child hadn't mattered to her so why should it now? She'd known how much he hated the smoky clubs she dragged him around when he should have been sleeping, and she'd turned a blind eye to the men who'd smacked him around when they'd had a skinful and were looking for trouble.

He'd turned his back on her. There was nothing more he wanted from her. *Almost nothing.* Nothing that would persuade him to see her again, he told himself furiously.

Yes, he'd turned his back on her, and he'd turn his back on Genie too. Just as soon as he could stop losing his mind every time she took her clothes off.

Chapter Twelve

'It's less than six weeks, Dee, and I've barely made a dent. I'm nowhere close to seeing how I can raise the sort of money needed to keep this place,' Genie said gloomily a few days later, her feet curled beneath her on the sofa. 'Maybe it's time to throw the towel in and hand the keys over.'

'It's not like you to be defeatist,' Deanna responded, dropping into the armchair.

Genie shrugged. It was hard to keep positive given the enormity of the task and the quickly diminishing timescale. 'Things around here are already so different without Uncle D.' She missed her uncle a great deal, seeing him on hops and catches around shows was nowhere near enough. It was difficult to acknowledge but good to know that he seemed happier than ever since he'd been living with Robin.

'You must miss him.' Deanna nodded, understanding, watching Genie closely. 'How are things with… you know who?' She jerked her head towards the presumed location of the man currently residing across the landing from Genie's front door.

Once more, Genie shrugged. 'You know how,' she said vaguely.

'Not really,' Deanna said patiently, clearly waiting for more.

Genie cast around for the best way to explain. 'It's a bit complicated,' she said, lamely.

'I'm smart,' Deanna said, wide-eyed. 'I can understand complicated things.'

'Not this you won't,' Genie said. 'I don't like him, he doesn't like me, and then every now and then we meet in the middle and rip each other's clothes off.'

Deanna laughed into her coffee mug. 'Well that's not complicated. It's chemistry. You don't have to like someone to sleep with them. It helps, but it's not a deal breaker.'

'I get that. But there's something going on with him, he really hates what I do for a living.'

'Male chauvinist?' Deanna suggested.

Genie shook her head. 'I don't think it's as simple as that. It's something more, but I can't put my finger on it.'

'Maybe he's a recovering sex addict or something.'

Knowing him as intimately as she did in that particular respect, Genie seriously doubted Abel was a man likely to attempt to recover from such an addiction if he were to have one.

'Who knows,' she murmured. 'Either way, he's an unwelcome disruption.'

'Is there absolutely no chance of getting him on side as an investor?' Deanna tried, ever the optimist.

It was Genie's turn to laugh.

Deanna's expression turned thoughtful. 'Not a prayer? You're totally sure? Because it seems to me that he's the only wealthy investor we know.'

'The last time I spoke to him I threw something at him and called him a fuckwit.'

Deanna grinned. 'Someone has some serious sucking up to do then.'

'Not a chance.'

'So what *is* the plan then?'

Genie rubbed her hands over her face, aware that her answer wasn't going to cut it. 'Just keep doing what I'm doing and hope for a miracle?'

'You better start rubbing that lamp a bit harder in that case, Genie-girl. You might get your three wishes.'

'I only need one,' she said flatly. 'I just want everything to go back to how it was.' She finished her coffee and slid the mug onto the table. 'And for Abel Kingdom to piss off back to Australia.'

'That's two wishes. And you'd probably miss the angry sex.'

Genie hated the suggestion that she'd miss anything whatsoever about Abel Kingdom when this was all over.

She slept badly that night and woke early with Deanna's words still resounding in her ears. Would it be better if she attempted some kind of truce with Abel? There was very little point in going over there and attempting to hoodwink him with false friendliness; it wasn't her style and he'd see through her in a heartbeat. But the fact was that he was going to be under this roof for the foreseeable future and being around him like this was exhausting. She was constantly wound up; he was putting her off her game.

Seizing the moment, because she felt that if she didn't do it right now, she'd lose her nerve, she walked purposefully to the door of her apartment, marched across the hall, and knocked on his door.

'Go away. It's the middle of the goddamn night,' Abel shouted, unwilling to get out of bed at the crack of dawn when he'd slept so badly.

'It's gone seven.'

Genie. Who else? He contemplated rolling over and going back to sleep, but if there was one thing he'd learned about the girl it was that she was tenacious. She'd probably knock on that door until her knuckles bled. Resigned, he yanked on his jeans and headed out of his room.

'Come to throw something else at me?' he said, lounging on the doorframe and trying to look disinterested. She was bare faced and wearing a white cotton slip, which unfortunately for him played right into his perfect fantasy of her. She looked as if she needed flowers threaded through her hair, like she'd stepped out of the pages of Pride and Prejudice. Pillageable.

'Only to make a suggestion,' she said simply. 'Can I come in?'

He stepped aside, noticing she was barefoot as she passed him, surrounding him with the clean scent of fresh water and subtle feminine shower gel. She had a unique way of playing with his head, the constant push and pull sent him into a tailspin. Showgirl. Innocent. Showgirl. Innocent. She didn't know it, but here, like this, she was most potent of all. He was already fighting the urge to pick her up and carry her to the bedroom.

Was she wearing anything underneath that thing? It had tiny buttons down the front, the kind that would bounce off the floorboards with a pleasurable ping if he took the fabric in his hands and pulled it open. She had to know what she looked like, all peaches and cream skin and her hair in waves down her back.

'Coffee?' he said, because he needed one himself.

She nodded and perched on a chair at his dining table. He moved around the kitchen, taking his time, pulling himself together. She waited quietly, not making small talk or even the tiniest wisecrack or jibe. What was coming next, he wondered? What role was she playing now?

At last, placing her coffee down, he took the next seat at the table and watched her.

'Out with it then,' he said, and she smiled a tentative smile that he knew would stay in his head for a while after she'd left.

'Well,' she began, and he could hear the nerves in her voice. 'I think we need a different approach.'

He wasn't sure what she meant. 'Go on.'

She looked a little nervous. Uncharacteristically so.

'I'm not going to throw things at you any more. Or call you names. Or fight with you all the time.'

'That just about sums up our entire acquaintance up to this point,' Abel said. 'Are you suggesting we avoid each other altogether?'

'No, not exactly,' she said slowly, her hands curled around

the mug on the table. 'I thought we could try being friends.'

'Friends?' he said.

'Or people who can get along with each other, at least,' she added.

Did she think he was so easily fooled?

'Are you trying to butter me up to stop me buying the theatre? Because it won't work, Beauty.'

'I'm not. And I'm not going to stop trying every trick in the book to stop you, but all this… this *other stuff* between us is wearing me out.'

Abel liked the idea of wearing her out very much, though he chose not to voice it.

'So what are you saying? You wanna do stuff like go to the movies instead?' Actually, scrap that. The idea of taking Genie to the movies made him think of being in a dark place and sliding his hand up her skirt.

'You should know that there's no way I'm going shoe shopping with you,' he said, flippant. 'Or painting your nails.' He glanced down at her coral pink toenails, and then back up the length of her body again. 'I don't mind having a crack at your bikini line though.'

She laughed easily, ignoring his crassness. 'I'm not sixteen, Abel. I don't expect you to swap secrets and come to the disco with me. I just want things to be calmer between us. The occasional cup of coffee.' She glanced down at her mug to illustrate the point.

'Okay,' he said, wondering if he could be friends with Genie. Back home he had several close female friends, but they weren't women he struggled to be around without getting hard. Sure, they were beautiful, just not his kind of beautiful. 'Let's try it. Why not? Lunch today?' he found himself adding. 'I'll cook for you.'

Her eyes opened a little wider. 'You cook?'

Abel nodded. He could cook. He'd had to fend for himself from a pretty early age.

'All right.' She looked nonplussed for a moment, then laughed with the lightest of shrugs. 'Lunch it is.'

Genie returned to her side of the hallway, unsure whether to be glad or not at how readily Abel had accepted her olive branch. Lunch. It brought a whole new meaning to keeping your friends close and your enemies closer.

Christ, he'd taken fresh-out-of-bed rumpled to a whole new level over there just now: sexy didn't even begin to cover how he'd looked in his clearly just-yanked-on jeans. He had a presence, a vitality, he was a big solid wall of Australian oh-my-God sexiness that made her throat constrict. She huffed out, dragging her hair back into a ponytail. Deanna was right. There was a basic sexual chemistry between them, as undeniable as breathing.

Unlike breathing though, Genie rather hoped that being attracted to each other was something she and Abel could make the decision to opt out of and survive.

Chapter Thirteen

'Stir fry?' Genie said enquiringly, taking a seat at Abel's dining table a little while later.

Abel set a plate down in front of Genie. 'I like healthy stuff.'

'Must be all that healthy outdoor living,' Genie smiled, spearing a prawn. 'Don't you usually barbecue these things?'

'I've been known to fire up the barbie every now and then,' Abel said, giving the phrase an ironic emphasis, pouring wine into Genie's glass and then his own. 'It's kind of a way of life over there. We spend more time outside in the sunshine.'

'You sound as if you love Australia,' she observed, taking pleasure in the way his face lit up when he talked about home.

Abel nodded. 'It's home. Our skies are wider. Our seas are bluer. The opportunities are bigger.' He paused, wistful. 'And the people are warmer. I'll never come back here to live.'

Genie mulled over what he'd said, understanding his accent more now. He'd been hard to place; mostly British, but every now and then he'd say something with an unmistakable Aussie twang. His love for his adopted home shone from both his face and his words. 'How old were you when you emigrated?'

A shadow passed over his features before he cleared it away with a shrug. 'Eighteen.'

Genie took a moment to savour the food; Abel made a mean stir fry. 'With your folks?'

There it was again, that shadow, lingering this time as he shook his head. 'No.'

It was such a concise answer, it left Genie with few avenues to keep the conversation going without pushing.

Abel picked up his wine glass and smiled before touching it to his lips.

'And you?' he said, sliding his glass back onto the table, his fingers lingering on the stem. 'How did you end up living here with your uncle?'

'My mother wasn't the maternal type. She left me on the theatre steps when I was a kid with a note asking Uncle Davey to look after me.' It was Genie's turn to reach for her wine. 'He always jokes I was like Paddington Bear but without the wellingtons.'

Abel was quiet for a second. 'That's a lot to ask of a man.'

'Uncle Davey might wear dresses and four inch heels but he's the strongest man I know.' Warmth spread through Genie's bones as she thought of her uncle. 'He never once made me feel like an inconvenience.'

'I'm guessing you don't have brothers and sisters then,' Abel said.

Genie shook her head. 'Although Deanna is as good as. I can't remember a time when she wasn't my best friend.'

Abel's eyebrows shifted slightly. 'Yeah. I'd noticed she's a little territorial.'

'Protective,' Genie corrected, amused. 'And you?' she said, laying her cutlery down. 'Any siblings?'

'Just me.' Abel's throat worked as he swallowed, drawing Genie's eyes to the golden skin at the neck of his tee shirt. He'd dressed casually for their lunch, still barefoot in his well-loved jeans and a faded tee. It was a look he worked well.

'Why do I get the feeling that you don't want to talk about this stuff?' she asked, sipping her wine.

'Because I don't want to talk about this stuff,' he said evenly. 'There's nothing to tell. Australia is my home. I have good friends and business is booming. End of story.'

He made it sound so clear-cut, so why did she feel as if he

were glossing over the important bits?

'Sounds good,' she said. 'You must miss the sunshine while you're here.'

'Is that your roundabout way of asking me when I'm going to go home and leave you in peace?'

She laughed. 'It wasn't, but seeing as you mention it...'

'You're out of luck, Beauty. I'm here for a while yet.'

Genie glanced down at her almost empty dinner plate, absorbing the information and trying to decide how it made her feel.

Abel stood and crossed to the open plan kitchen, returning with the wok in his hand.

'More?' He gestured towards her plate and looked pleased when she accepted seconds.

'This is delicious,' she said. 'Who taught you to cook?'

'The TV,' he replied smoothly.

Not his mother then, Genie surmised, although she didn't pry about his family for a second time. He'd made it pretty clear that it wasn't a subject he wanted to talk about.

'Well, you're way ahead of me,' she said. 'I'm hopeless.'

'I'm sure you have your own talents,' he murmured, refilling their wine glasses before glancing up, a little abashed, then adding, 'I didn't actually mean that to sound like a come-on.'

Genie concentrated on eating her food to avoid answering him for a moment. He certainly didn't appreciate her talents on stage. 'I believe you.'

A small, genuine smile curved his mouth. 'Thank you.'

It was a moment of understanding that wasn't usual for them.

'It's hard to place you from your accent,' she said, moving the conversation along. 'Which part of the UK are you from originally?'

She'd thought it a fairly innocuous question, so was surprised by the dark cloud that wiped the easy smile from his face.

'London,' he said, and then shoved his chair back and

gathered the plates.

'Really?' Genie said, surprised to find he was a native of her city. He seemed anything but comfortable here. 'Whereabouts?'

Abel walked away with the plates stacked in his hands. 'So, what are they?' he said, making Genie frown with confusion at the spectacular change of topic.

'What are what?'

He loaded the plates into the dishwasher and then kicked the door up into place.

'Your talents,' he said, and this time it sounded very much as if he did mean it as a come-on. Or possibly as a distraction, and if that was his intention, it worked.

Genie's pulse kicked up instantly, because the look in his eye had turned predatory.

'I'm pretty good at reading people,' she said softly. 'Knowing when they're hiding something.'

He regarded her assessingly. 'Dessert?'

'Did you make it?'

'Especially for you,' he said.

'Oh… then, yes. Yes please.'

Abel nodded and turned away to the fridge. Genie watched the defined muscles of his back work through his flimsy tee shirt then flicked her eyes to the ceiling to slow the train of thought that was headed right down inside the waistband of Abel's jeans. She knew what lay beyond those buttons, and how much pleasure he could give her with his hands.

Laying a plate on the table between them, Abel looked almost self-conscious for a second. 'Your uncle is one kitsch bastard.'

Genie understood him a second or two later when he returned to the table with her Uncle Davey's chocolate fondue pot and long silver forks. On the plate lay ripe, glistening strawberries, chunks of golden pineapple and plump pink marshmallows ready for dipping.

'Wow,' she laughed, picking up one of the forks from beside

the cast iron chocolate pot. 'It's been a while since this thing saw daylight. Years, even.'

Abel shrugged. 'Why does that not surprise me? It's a pain in the ass.' He picked up a fork and waved it over the plate. 'Ladies first.'

She considered the options and then speared a strawberry, leaning over the pot a little to dip it into the warm chocolate. Abel followed her lead, stabbing a chunk of pineapple and dunking it in the pot.

'Oh my God,' she murmured after she'd eaten it. It was chocolate heaven. 'I'd forgotten how good it is.' She went in for a second time, swirling a marshmallow until it was fully coated. 'This is officially my favourite dessert ever.'

She closed her eyes and savoured it, and when she opened them found Abel watching her and looking quietly pleased with himself.

'You've impressed yourself,' she said.

He lifted a shoulder and grinned as he pushed his fork through a marshmallow. 'Maybe a little bit.'

He cursed as the enamel handle on his fork snapped and dropped to the floor. He bent to pick it up and laid it on the table.

'It *is* pretty old,' Genie said ruefully. 'Here.' She dipped a marshmallow and held her fork out towards him. 'You can share mine.'

He looked uncertain for a moment, as if he wasn't sure if she expected him to take the whole fork or just the marshmallow. She wasn't really sure herself, if she was totally honest. After a tiny pause he moved towards her and parted his lips, and she followed his lead and slid the marshmallow into his mouth. It was undeniably sexy. Not platonic at all.

She took a moment to recover her composure, sliding a chunk of pineapple into the chocolate and eating it slowly.

'More?' she said, hovering the fork over the plate and looking his way. He nodded, and she selected a ruby red strawberry to load up with melted chocolate. He watched her eyes as she offered the fruit to his lips, moving his head forward a fraction to take the strawberry with his teeth. Christ. She wanted his mouth to close around her nipple just like that.

Abel took the fork gently from her fingers and speared another strawberry, dipping it before sliding his chair right up close to Genie's. His other hand rested along the back of her seat as he moved the fruit towards her lips. Genie suddenly didn't care at all that he'd shifted the goalposts swiftly from friendship to flirtation - he had a way of making her intentions and resolutions insignificant, drifting tantalisingly out of her grasp.

She'd get them back in a minute, just as soon as she'd eaten that delicious looking fruit. Genie felt sudden kinship with Eve; the temptation really *was* impossible to resist.

It was especially difficult to resist when Abel chose not to slip the strawberry directly into her mouth but instead slid it along her parted lips, smearing chocolate wherever it touched. His fingertips brushed her shoulder and his thigh lay warm against hers, and he watched her mouth as he finally pushed the fruit between her slick lips. She barely tasted it as it moved down her throat, because Abel laid the fork down and slid his hand into her hair, holding her face a breath away from his.

'You've got a little chocolate just… here,' he whispered, tracing the tip of his tongue along her upper lip. Genie could barely breathe.

Abel closed his eyes, making a low sound of pleasure in his throat, and Genie felt it all the way down to her groin.

'And here,' he said, turning his attention to her lower lip, licking, grazing his teeth against her softness. Imprisoned lightly by his hand at her jaw, Genie opened her mouth to let his tongue in, thoroughly under the spell of his barely-there hands and his unhurried kiss. It was the kind of kiss designed to draw a line in the sand and invite you to cross it; come over, come and be with me, it's decadent and sensual and meltingly good on the other side. Come to me.

And she did, because it would have taken superwoman to resist Abel in full on seduction mode. He had a way about him, an easy confidence, an assured way of touching her that said, relax, I'm a man who knows what he's doing and it's going to blow your goddamn mind.

Genie slid her arms around the breadth of his shoulders, arching into him when he slid both hands into her hair and held her steady. His body angled over hers, pinning her to the chair, making her wish she was pinned beneath him on the floor, or in bed, or anywhere that involved his body over hers. And then she wasn't pinned, because Abel suddenly lifted her from the chair to straddle him, his cock hard and straining against his jeans between her legs.

She'd dressed carefully, opting for a casual, hopefully friendly look in her most comfy denim mini and layered pink and white vest tops. Abel peeled her vests over her head and unclipped her bra in the space of time it took her to realise she was on his lap, turning her on even more with his impatience to get her naked. She knew the feeling, and reached down to drag his tee shirt off and throw it down on top of her clothes, craving the heat of his skin on hers.

He was a contrast to her in every way. Hard where she was soft, tanned where she was pale, but when it came to being hot for each other they were in complete unison. Abel held her in place with his warm, strong hands around her ribs, dipping his head to trail scorching kisses from her shoulder to the hollow at the base of her neck. Genie was untroubled by any thoughts of resisting him; he was just too delicious not to indulge in.

He seemed to think the same of her, because he reached behind her and dipped his fingers into the warm chocolate then drew them down her neck, creating lines for him to lick off. He was oh so thorough about it too, tipping her head back to expose her properly to him.

When he re-dipped his fingers, Genie watched his gaze drop to her breasts and then back up to meet hers, the vaguest hint of chocolate on his full lips from her neck.

The suspense of waiting for his touch was almost as pleasurable as his touch itself, as was the achingly sexy look in his dark eyes. They spent so much of their time crossing swords that it intensified these moments when the defences came down. He looked hungry, as if he couldn't decide whether to smear her in chocolate or just eat her whole.

Genie dragged in a sharp breath when he reached out and drew slow circles around her nipples, concentric, getting smaller, tighter, still looking in her eyes, watching her reactions.

'You look pretty fucking filthy,' he said, dropping his gaze once more to her breasts in his hands.

'So clean me up,' she said, holding his gaze, her breath too quick in her chest.

Abel dropped his head and did as he was told, sucking her nipple into his mouth, licking, pulling, his closed eyes rendering him unreadable. She pushed her fingers into the thickness of his hair as he moved to her other breast, still holding her flesh in his hands, massaging her as he worked her slowly up and up into a frenzy.

He dragged his open mouth back up the length of her neck to her ear, sending delicious shivers down her spine.

'If I smear chocolate over your clit, will you ask me to lick that clean too?'

Genie moved restlessly over his swollen crotch, in no doubt at all that she would. She was hot, and flustered, and needy. He'd turned her on with his mouth and his words, and her body had flicked over into that state where only one thing would satisfy it.

Sex. Or in Genie's case, fiery, intense fucking with Abel Kingdom. There were no conscious thought patterns here; it was all about instinct and primal, animal needs.

Reaching for his jeans, she flicked the buttons open and pushed them down as far as she could, freeing his iron-hard cock into her waiting hand.

'If I smear chocolate over your cock, will you ask me to lick that clean too?' she managed to say, almost yelping when he slid a hand between her legs and stroked his fingertips over the scrap of silk that passed for her knickers. She might have dressed casually for their lunch, but she'd worn killer underwear all the same.

'You can bet your fucking last breath on it, lady,' Abel said, sweeping the silk aside and sliding his fingers between her lips.

Genie gasped, taking a moment to open her eyes and connect with him, leaning in to kiss him, the brush of open mouth against open mouth making their touches all the more intimate. She matched her speed with his; a languid, meltingly erotic build.

'Take your jeans off,' she whispered, helping him push them down then twisting to scoop some of the blood-warm chocolate in her fingers.

Abel watched her, and then meshed his fingers with her slippery ones, covering his own in chocolate too.

He moaned when Genie's fingers curled around his shaft, a low, intensely sexual rumble that pushed her closer to the edge before he'd even touched her. And then he did, warm slippery fingers smearing chocolate where chocolate had never been before. They sat for a couple of intense, breathless minutes, stroking, rubbing, fingering, discovering.

Abel held her head to his and urged his kiss as deep as he could go, his tongue restless and insistent inside her mouth.

'I need to taste you.' It was a statement of fact. 'Here.' He moved his fingers over her clitoris.

Genie pumped his shaft steadily. 'I want you in my mouth,' she whispered, torn between the need to give pleasure and take it. Was there even a difference, right now?

Abel's arms moved around her, lifting her and then sinking to the floor, laying her down and dragging her skirt and underwear off at the same time. Twisting to lie the opposite way to her, he opened her legs and pulled her onto her side so he could lay his head on her inner thigh. His arm wound over her hip, he buried his face between her legs, opening her folds with his fingers, tasting her, licking her clean in the filthiest possible way, suckling on her clitoris until she whimpered the only word in her head. *Abel.*

In return, Genie feasted on him. His big, beautiful, chocolate smeared cock filled her mouth and then some, delicious and addictive. She slid him in deep and then moved her head back, loving his low moans of pleasure and the way his arms banded more tightly around her when she sank her mouth all the way down over him again. He massaged the cheeks of her ass, his mouth and hands everywhere until she was one hot mess of nerve endings waiting for him to give her what she was desperate for. Abel pushed her knee out, spreading her wide, exposing her as much as she could be to his eyes and his mouth.

'Abel… please,' she murmured, her fingers sliding over his cock.

He kissed the softness of her inner thighs, holding her folds open as he drew his head back a little to blow cooling air across her clitoris. Could you come just from fresh air? Genie thought it was highly goddamn likely as his breath whispered over her; cooling, drying, and making her throb.

'Please what, Beauty?' he said, his mouth a fraction from where she needed it to be, his voice less controlled than usual. 'Please tongue my beautiful, swollen clit?' he suggested for her, and the explicitness of his words turned her inside out. 'You look fucking amazing.'

He kneaded her backside, his fingertips brushing up between her legs, dipping just inside her. His cock strained in her hands, and she knew that when she took him into her mouth again he'd come there and then.

Abel blew softly again, and then his mouth fastened over her, sudden and hot and wet, his tongue quick, sure and relentless over her clit as he pushed his fingers inside her. He held her against him when she squirmed in shock, and started to thrust as soon as she took the length of his cock into her mouth.

His fingers bit into her ass as she came hard against the flat of his tongue, his body tense and spilling into her mouth as his hips jerked. Genie had never known euphoric intensity like it; and now it was over, such a slow, sweet come down. Her whole body had lit up for him, and as he mouthed slow, open kisses over her sex she laid her head on his thigh and savoured the sensations still rolling through her body.

'So hot,' he murmured against her warmth, his words vibrating richly over her flesh. 'So wet, Beauty, and so fucking delicious.'

Genie let him take charge, let him push her further when she'd expected him to let her come down, feeling the incredible sensations starting to tingle and build all over again. He was so meltingly good, holding her open with his massaging fingertips and loving her slowly with the erotic drag of his tongue now flat against her flesh, and then tracing intricate, barely-there patterns over her clit. He had her high, drugged on him, with the intense sensation of her second orgasm hovering on the edges of her consciousness.

It was coming, she knew it and he seemed to know too. Splaying his hands on her thighs, he opened her as wide as she could be and took her clit into his mouth, sucking it in deep. Genie's stomach muscles contracted hard, raising her shoulders from the floor, the strength of her orgasm curling her body up towards Abel. She buried her hands in his hair; clutching at him, gasping, shuddering. Every release this man gave her seemed better than the last. How long could that go on for before she died of pleasure?

Abel slid up her body, kissing all of the skin he passed on the way back to her mouth.

'You're welcome,' he said, the smallest of self-satisfied smiles on his lips as he lowered his head and kissed her lingeringly. His dark hair fell forward and brushed Genie's face, and she swept it back with her fingers.

'That was unexpected,' she whispered, a little shakily.

'You mean you don't do this with all your *friends* after a lunch date?' he said, lifting his head and looking down at her. 'You should.'

She rolled her eyes. 'I didn't mean for this to happen today,' she said, conflicted.

He shrugged, unfazed. 'Don't beat yourself up. Women often lose control around me.' She wasn't sure if he was mocking her, or himself.

'Abel, I mean it, okay? I thought it'd make things easier if we tried to be friends, not even more complicated.' Those conscious thought patterns were beginning to return.

'Why is it more complicated if we fuck sometimes?' he asked. 'I can separate business from pleasure if you can. I'm still buying your theatre.'

The simple clarity of his words came as no real surprise, and Genie wasn't sure whether to feel impressed or offended. She hadn't had sex with him to try to persuade him not to buy the place. She'd had sex with him because he'd turned her on so much that all common sense had left the building, but that wasn't really good enough, was it? Was she going to melt every time he glanced her way?

'And I'm still going to stop you getting your hands on it,' she said, deciding to match his boldness.

'You don't seem so bothered about stopping me getting my hands on you,' he said, palming her breast.

Genie stilled beneath him. 'When you say separate business from pleasure, I'm guessing you mean you're separating what I do for business from what we do for pleasure?'

He studied her face, frowning. 'Just so you're really clear, Genie, I'm fucking my neighbour here, not the stripper downstairs. What you choose to do down there is nothing to do with this.'

Genie needed to have this discussion with him when they were dressed again; it was too much to listen to him denigrate her lifestyle while he stroked her lust-hardened nipples. Wriggling out from under him, she reached for her clothes and began to drag them back on.

'You know what, Abel?' she said a moment later, standing up and winding her mussed up hair into a knot at the back of her neck. 'I don't think I can compartmentalise quite as effectively as you obviously can.'

He stood up and stepped into his jeans. 'Why are you making such a big deal about it now?'

The fact that he sounded genuinely perplexed served only to annoy Genie more.

'Because it *is* a big deal to me.'

'I don't see why. Upstairs you're the girl next door. Normal clothes. Normal make-up. No fucking glitter. It's just you and me. Downstairs you're…' he searched around for the right words. 'You're none of those things.'

He really knew how to press her buttons, both sexually and emotionally. Genie's blood literally bubbled faster in her veins.

'So what exactly are you saying here, Abel? I'm your upstairs angel, downstairs whore?'

Frustration was written all over his face. 'Not exactly, no, but if the cap fits…' He gave up on the sentence, pulling his tee shirt over his head.

She stared at him, wondering how he could make her feel so good and so bad within the space of a few minutes.

'It doesn't fit,' she said, quietly. 'It constricts me, and it hurts.'

And with that, she picked up her shoes and left him there, frowning and scrubbing his hands through his hair.

Chapter Fourteen

As texts went, Deanna's message a couple of mornings later was definitely brimming with intrigue.

'Possible MAJOR development. Hold all calls, am coming over now and bringing a guest. DO NOT LEAVE THE BUILDING.'

Genie read it twice over, looking for clues hidden among the short sentences. Who was Deanna bringing over? Had she found them a business angel to swoop in and save the day? Desperate hope fizzed in her gut at the idea of possibly, maybe, somehow being able to hang onto her beloved theatre. In recent days she'd started to feel that it was hopeless… and now she barely dared hope that someone might be about to throw her a lifeline.

Genie would have had a hard time admitting it, but there was a second, less admirable reason now for saving the theatre. She wanted to beat Abel Kingdom. She wanted to show him that feathers and glitter and rhinestones and passion could trump muscle and hard, ruthless business.

She'd avoided him since their lunch date earlier in the week, still furious with him for being so damn pigheaded. She'd been wrong to think there was any possibility of friendship between them. She might have to live under the same roof as him for a few more weeks, but the day was coming when she'd be able to send him on his way. Hell, she'd even do his packing for him. Anything to get him out of her home and her life, he was screwing her up with his hot body and mean spirit. He blurred all sensible, straight lines. She didn't like him one bit but he made her hot in a way no man ever had before. She didn't share any of his beliefs and yet she wanted him to force him to share hers, or at least to open his mind to a different way of thinking. But she now knew that he was intractable.

Deanna arrived as promised, with a woman in tow. Unreasonably, Genie was disappointed: she'd kind of anticipated a guy in a suit, and in the fantasy she'd happily entertained just now in the shower, he'd had a chequebook in his hand. This woman looked like one of Deanna's photography student friends, dressed down in jeans and sneakers with a camera slung low around her neck and her pale hair pulled back in a messy bun.

'Genie, this is Ada.' Deanna made the introduction, almost hopping from one foot to the other with barely contained excitement. Genie shot her friend a quick, curious look as Ada surveyed the auditorium, then she stuck her hand out with a smile.

'I'm Genie,' she said, taking the other woman's outstretched hand. 'It's nice to meet you.'

Ada nodded, her eyes still roaming the theatre. 'This is quite the place you have here,' she said, and right away Genie detected the rounded American accent behind her admiring tone. Ada turned her gaze to Deanna. 'You weren't lying when you said it was old school,' she grinned, her hands on her hips and her face full of wonder as she took the old place in. 'It's just beautiful.'

Deanna nodded and then looked at Genie triumphantly. 'Ada is a location scout for Dalton Productions.'

It wasn't at all what Genie had anticipated her friend would say. She'd heard of Dalton Productions, of course she had, she hadn't spent the last ten years living under a rock. They were one of the biggest movie producers in Hollywood, she'd grown up seeing their company logo emblazoned on the screen before scores of blockbuster films at the cinema.

'Sounds an interesting job,' Genie said carefully, her mind

alight with hope and possibilities.

'It sure is,' Ada agreed, picking up her camera and looking through the lens with one eye squinted shut. 'Bali, New Zealand, Moscow…it takes me all over, I love it.'

Deanna clutched her hands together in a move that said *I want your life* and spoke a little breathlessly. 'Dalton are looking for a theatre to film a movie in later this year. And I thought this place might fit the bill.'

Ada nodded, readjusting the lens of the camera. 'It's a sweeping romantic saga set around the production of a musical during the second world war,' she explained, lifting the camera to her eye again to check it. 'Mind if I take a look around on my own? I want to get some close ups on the architectural details. I might be a while.'

'Go for it,' Genie said, finding her voice, opening her hands wide and smiling. 'Go anywhere you need to.' She gestured upwards. 'The carving on the boxes is especially beautiful.'

Deanna and Genie watched Ada make her way out into the foyer and then sat down on the edge of the stage, their legs dangling.

'What's going on, Dee?' Genie whispered.

Deanna grinned. 'I know, crazy, right? I saw this article in my monthly photographers' magazine about Dalton Productions, a big splashy double page spread. Anyway, it mentioned Ada and her fabulous job as a location scout, and after I died of jealousy I emailed her and told her about the theatre.'

'You never told me you did that,' Genie said, leaning her shoulder against Deanna's and swinging her legs. They looked like a couple of kids skimming rocks off the end of a pier rather than two women trying to produce a miracle out of hope, thin air and glitter.

'I didn't really think anything would come of it,' Deanna admitted, bright-eyed. 'But then she emailed me and said it must be fate because they were actually looking for somewhere in London exactly like this and could she come over and see it in person. Oh my God, Genie! I didn't tell you in case she changed her mind, but she didn't and now she's here. Isn't that bizarre!'

Genie nodded. Bizarre was a good word for it. She still hadn't quite taken it in. 'So... how does it work then?'

'That's the best bit,' Deanna said out of the side of her mouth, looking out for Ada. 'If they decide this place fits the bill, then they hire it lock stock and barrel for the duration of the shoot.'

'Which is... ?'

'Four months! And here's the even better bit. She mentioned a figure that would give you enough money to buy this place and go on a world cruise with the change! Honestly, G, I tried to look cool but I'm not sure I pulled it off... I practically wet myself!'

Genie's mind raced at the news. It was a potential game changer. 'I can't believe it,' she murmured.

'It's not definite yet,' Deanna cautioned, clearly fearing that Genie would be too crushed if it didn't come off.

'I know, I know.' Genie held Deanna's hand. 'Thank you Dee. Even if it doesn't happen, I love that you're trying so hard.'

Deanna squeezed her fingers and grinned. 'Imagine it though G... Jesus, I hope Ryan Gosling is in it. I'll be here every bloody day! In fact I'll move in!'

Genie laughed. 'You can have Uncle Davey's flat when we kick God's Gift out.'

Both girls fell silent. 'I can't believe we might actually pull this off,' Deanna said quietly.

Genie nodded. The idea of being able to run upstairs and victoriously tell Abel Kingdom to book his flight home held a lot of appeal, but then... gah. But then nothing. She pushed any feelings of anything other than elation firmly down and out of her head. Better to concentrate all of her thoughts and hope on the slender American woman clicking away on her camera out in the foyer.

Spirits amongst the Divine Girls soared when they heard the - for now - confidential news about the movie, and it seemed to rub off on both their performances and the theatre's books. Their sensual, high energy shows were very often sell-outs, and the theatre's profits grew healthier by the day. It wouldn't be enough on its own to trouble Abel Kingdom, but if the movie offer came through then they'd be home and dry.

Genie didn't mention the lifeline to her uncle: the thought of getting his hopes up only to dash them again was too much to bear. So she hugged her secret to herself, and slept with her fingers crossed and dreamed big dreams of the theatre's rosy future. Subtle renovations would be the order of the day, nothing too noticeable, just enough to let the old girl shine as she really deserved to. The movie Ada had outlined called for a place with faded grandeur, which was pretty much exactly what they had at the moment. Once the movie was done with and when funds permitted, Genie was going to see to it that Theatre Divine went all out from faded to fabulous.

Across the landing, Abel stewed in his own juices. He'd been avoiding Genie since the fondue incident, in fact he'd thrown the whole fondue set out the same day, as if it were personally to blame for the disastrous way their lunch date had ended. He hadn't intended to call Genie a whore five minutes after throwing her on the floor and eating chocolate from the most intimate parts her body, it had just kind of happened that way. Why couldn't she see the difference?

How could he explain that when she donned her disguise of feathers, glitter and rhinestones, she covered the real woman he was attracted to? How hard was it for her to understand that strippers didn't turn him on? It was as if she didn't see the distinction between the two sides of her life, and she was offended that he did.

Glancing outside and frowning at the gathering clouds overhead, he grabbed his jacket and slammed his way out of the theatre. The forecasters hadn't been wrong with their stormy predictions for the day ahead on the radio. Rain, rain and more fucking infernal rain. Grey streets under grey skies in a city full of grey people. His skin itched as he walked the familiar route towards his childhood home. He didn't have a conscious plan. Well he did, really, but because he hadn't reached the point of being able to face it directly he told himself he was just going for a walk to blow away the cobwebs.

Cobwebs. That was exactly how he felt, as if invisible nets were being wrapped around him, tightening, constricting his breathing until he broke into a sweat and battled for air. He wanted to go home. He longed for the clean air and sunshine, for the warmth and familiarity of the friends he counted as family in the absence of the real thing.

Maybe that was why he'd let this thing with Genie get so tangled up: he was on his own here, and she staved off the spectre of his childhood. Even if they were at loggerheads, she was a distraction, a preoccupation – perhaps an obsession. She made him forget the bad stuff lurking around all the corners in this drab city. He didn't look at London and see cosmopolitan or vibrant. He'd never got past seeing it through his own eleven-year-old eyes, a place where he wasn't safe, where people lied for convenience, and where love didn't count for anything.

Love. It was a word he'd struggled with his whole adult life, because it was something no one had bothered to teach him as a child. He'd arrived in Australia hardened, and much as he'd embraced his new life, love wasn't part of his mindset. He'd dated, sure, but always backed off when women wanted more from him than he had to give. Sex was one thing; he was more than happy to share his body, but emotional intimacy didn't sit easy with him. It wasn't that he didn't believe in love, or anything quite so dramatic. It was more that he didn't particularly see the benefit of it, nor did he consider himself eligible for it in the long term.

If your own mother can't love you, who can?

And suddenly he was there, dragging his feet as he drew closer to the row of terraces, shabby two-up two-downs lived in by downtrodden people. And his mother. Head down, hands in his pockets and shoulders hunched, he glanced up through his lashes towards her windows. It was a little before ten in the morning; early, by her standards in any case. Predictably, the curtains were still drawn downstairs, and Abel found himself caught between relief and irritation. Had he hoped to catch her up and ready for a visitor, or maybe just leaving the house, so as to force a meeting without him needing to knock on the door? Why was he even here?

He didn't know what the hell he was going to say to her, he just knew that he couldn't go back to Australia with unfinished business. What was the point in opening a gym around the corner from here, in stamping his authority and success on the area if he wasn't going to see her? How could he erase the pencil stroke memories of a slight, dark haired boy in charity shop clothes from the history of these streets if he didn't face down the reason he'd fallen through the cracks, become the invisible boy for so many years?

Movement caught his eye. The curtains were being opened. He walked on quickly, unreasonable panic rising in his throat. He made it to the end of the street and rounded the corner before bending double and throwing up in a drain.

Leaning shamefacedly on the nearest wall afterwards, horrified by the strength and physicality of his reaction, he caught his breath and pulled himself together. This wasn't okay. This wasn't how he'd expected to feel. He'd planned to come back here, to walk right on up that no doubt still cracked path to her front door and bang on it. To let her see his good clothes and decent shoes and know that she hadn't broken him. He'd been back once before to offer her his help; this time he wanted only to show her how far he'd come without her.

Standing there, breathing in, breathing out, Abel grew slowly more and more angry. Angry with his mother for what she'd made him, and angry with himself for not proving her wrong.

Breathe in. Breathe out. He concentrated on the steady tempo, regulating himself, calming down. He wasn't a kid any more, and this wasn't his home. He didn't have to be here, but the fact was that he needed to come back one last time or else he'd be forever tied, bound by dirty ropes of self-doubt holding him back.

Lifting his head, he looked one way towards the main road, and then back over his shoulder towards the nondescript street he'd grown up on. After a long moment, he doubled back on himself and set off with a purposeful stride towards his mother's house.

Back at the theatre, Genie was practically jumping for joy. Fresh off the phone with Ada from Dalton Productions, she sat down hard on the sofa with her hands flat against her hot cheeks that ached from smiling. Ada had fed back all of her findings on the theatre to the team at Dalton and it had been a unanimous decision - Theatre Divine was perfect for the movie and they'd like to get the ball rolling on contract negotiations as soon as possible. It meant closing down for a while for filming to take place, but how exciting would that be! And then the theatre would at last be back in the family, saved and secure, and she and Uncle D could go about the pleasurable business of restoring it to its well-deserved former glory.

She picked up her phone, desperate to tell him the good news, and then cut it off again before it rang out. She'd wait until the contracts came through, just to be double certain.

There was one person who she *wasn't* going to wait to tell though. Abel goddamn Kingdom. She jumped up and headed for her door, a ball of euphoric energy. Brace yourself mister, I'm about to blindside you and you didn't even see me coming.

Abel had been right about that path. It was still cracked, and what might have been a small patch of grass beside it was a mess of weeds and clumps of dry, bare earth. No change there then. He'd told himself that he was going to walk along it without faltering, and when he got the few steps further to the door he was going to raise his fist and knock on it hard. It was that or slink away like a coward, and of all the things that she'd made him, a coward wasn't one of them.

The paint was peeling on the door, as it always had been, and the knocker was long gone. Abel swallowed hard and then knocked, three sharp raps that said: *I'm not afraid.*

He knew better than to expect her to answer quickly. Right about now she'd be glancing at the mantel clock in her room and wondering who might be knocking this early, whether she could be bothered to get up just to turn away an electricity meter reader or someone in a cheap suit selling religion door to door. She was more accustomed to late night callers.

Movement through the opaque glass panes told him she'd decided to answer the door. He swallowed hard and pushed his hands through his hair before shoving them both in the pockets of his leather jacket and pushing his shoulders back. This was it, then.

Genie banged on a different door, the one opposite her own on the top floor of the theatre.

'Hey,' she called out, after her knock met only silence. 'I know you're in there, so you may as well open up.'

She listened to the stillness, then banged again, irritated.

'Open the door, Abel. I need to talk to you.'

Nothing at all. 'Fine,' she called out, eventually. 'Fine. Have it your own way, but just for the record, ignoring me is pretty fucking childish. I'm over here whenever you're ready. And you should know… I have *news*.'

She accentuated her words heavily, hoping to entice him out of his lair and failing, much to her annoyance. If it hadn't been for the fact that she'd have been exposing her own childish streak, she'd have delivered a good kick to his door before turning on her heel and stomping back into her own apartment, thwarted.

Abel watched his mother's face carefully as she opened the door. He had the advantage of the element of surprise to put him in the driving seat, to begin with at least. He badly needed to stay in it, to stay in charge of this situation without slamming his foot down on the accelerator and smashing himself into more pieces than he knew how to put back together.

Her initial, bland expression told him that she didn't recognise him straight away, and the suspicious frown that followed soon after told him that she had. She didn't say anything, and after a second her eyebrows moved up, a silent question. *What the hell do you want?*

'Can I come in?' he said shortly, lifting his shoulders in the slightest of shrugs.

She paused, considering, then swung the door open and walked away from him up the hallway. Abel took a last breath of morning air, and then ducked his head under the lintel and followed his mother inside his old home.

'I take it this is just a flying visit,' she said, her voice flat as she turned to face him in the small living room. So little had changed since his time here. Replaced cushions, maybe, and an incongruously girlish pink notepad on the floor beside the sofa. 'Because your room isn't your room any more. I use it for junk.'

He watched her reach for her cigarettes from beside the over stuffed letter-rack, the same place as always, and then go through the ritual of lighting up. She held the packet out towards him, lazy mockery in her eyes. The same eyes as his own. Did he make people feel the way she could just with a glance? He sincerely hoped not.

He towered over her, and she flicked an imperious hand towards the sofa to bring him down to eye level. Abel looked around the gloomy, claustrophobic room with an inward sigh and opted for a dining chair at the small table near the window. His mother sat down opposite him, her heavy glass ashtray and cigarettes lined up on the table in front of her.

'So, to what do I owe the pleasure, Abel?'

She couldn't have made the fact that he was unwelcome more plain. In a perverse way, it made it easier. They were on the same page. The question he'd come to ask lingered in his parched mouth. This wasn't a social call and there was no place for social niceties. He was here now, and he didn't plan on coming back again. Out with it. He had nothing to lose.

'I want to know who my father is.'

He wasn't sure how to categorise the sound his mother made. Half laugh, half cough of surprise, and her lips curled into a slow, sarcastic smile as she looked down and tapped the lengthening ash from her cigarette.

'Why?'

He lifted one shoulder. 'Why not?'

'You won't get his kidney if you're dying.' She looked him over as she dragged deeply on the cigarette. 'Or mine, for that matter.'

Abel was fine with that. He'd rather die than accept any part of his mother's smoke-addled body. She seemed smaller than ever, more pinched around the mouth and lined around the eyes. Some women he knew in their fifties could pass for being in their thirties; his mother seemed to have gone the other way.

'I'm not dying,' he said. 'I just want to know who he is.'

She blew smoke out and set her features in an arrangement that might have been an attempt at regret. Or defiance. Or mockery. He just couldn't tell.

'I can't help you. I don't have a clue who he was.' She didn't look at all bothered. 'He could have been one of quite a few at the time.'

Was she lying? He couldn't tell that either. It was entirely possible that she didn't know, but all the same he'd hoped for a different answer. It was something that had begun to weigh on his mind more and more. He'd let himself become preoccupied with his past, with his mother, and with London, and the only way he could see to get it out of his system had been to come here and win. Win so categorically that whenever he thought of

London in the future he'd think only of his triumph rather than his childhood. Ripping the theatre apart and placing a clean, gleaming gym in its place was part of it. Facing his mother was part of it. And finding his father was the final piece of the jigsaw. Maybe, if he turned out to be a decent man, it would mean Abel was a decent man too. He didn't see any of himself in the woman opposite, besides her eyes.

'Still rolling in it?' she asked, her words loaded with scorn.

'I'm doing okay,' he said. He'd learned his lesson well the last time he'd come here and tried to help. Back then he'd been naive enough to try to think the best of her and hope she'd think the best of him back. This time he knew better. She wasn't asking in order to feel any sense of pride in her son. She was asking him so she could look down her nose out of some vastly misplaced inverted snobbery.

She snorted, stubbing out her cigarette and almost immediately lighting a second.

'My son the big shot,' she mocked.

Abel felt his hackles rise. 'What's so wrong with me doing well, mum?'

She shook her head, her lips turned down in a disinterested grimace. 'What are you really here for? To dirty your expensive shoes on my carpets?'

Abel thought of the years in old, ill-fitting shoes and bit back the angry words that filled his head. If he started, he wasn't sure he'd ever be able to stop.

'Tell me who he is and I'll go.'

She rolled her eyes. 'I've told you once. I don't know.'

'Think harder. Was there anyone special? Anyone besides your...' he cast around for a word that didn't make his mother sound like a prostitute. '...Your usual friends?'

She opened her eyes wide at this. 'So polite. You've got me to thank for that.'

He had nothing to be grateful to the woman opposite him for, yet still he didn't bite.

'Is his name on my birth certificate?' He knew the answer to that, of course he had checked years before, but he asked anyway.

'Australia's rubbed off on you. Just listen to your voice.' Her nose wrinkled with distaste. She mocked him again with an awful parody of his accent. 'Father unknown.' She laughed, contemptuous as she mimed a tick in the box in the air between them.

Abel scrubbed a hand over his jaw. 'Do you need money?'

He watched her eyes narrow before she looked down to stub out her cigarette.

'Are you suggesting that money might improve my memory, Abel?'

He shrugged. The gloves were off. 'Will it?'

'Haven't we been here before? You flash your money around and expect me to be impressed. I'm not interested in your fancy lifestyle or your bulging bank account. Nothing was ever good enough for you, was it? I scrimped to put food on your table and you left me at the first possible chance you had.'

'I came back for you,' he said, stung by the injustice and her selective memory.

'Too little too late, son,' she spat, more rattled than he'd seen her. What right did she have to her indignation?

'And now you come around here asking about your father, as if you think he's going to be some knight in shining armour rather than some two bit nobody who wouldn't give a stuff about you,' she said, her cold eyes mocking him again. 'What do you expect to happen, Abel? You're going to find out it's the bloody Prince of Wales, go and knock on his door and be welcomed in with open arms? Get your head out of the clouds, son. They were all good-for-nothings, so either way, the apple didn't fall far from the tree.'

Abel felt every word like a slap, and tried to filter out the insults from the truths scattered amongst them.

'So do you know who he is?' He tried again, keeping his voice even.

137

Her eyes flashed. 'He's probably dead.'

It was Abel's turn to mock. 'I don't believe you. You do know. Tell me his name.'

Her face was resolute. This was her only power, and she wasn't giving it up. 'No.' She shook her head. 'Believe whatever you want. You'll never know. Maybe I do, maybe I don't.'

He stared at her, knowing he had nothing to offer that she wanted. She was playing a power game, putting him in his place, keeping him down, as she always had. He realised with a sudden cold drench of conviction that she really didn't know. She was just toying with him, enjoying withholding a real answer of any kind. There was no big secret. It was as ugly and mundane a truth as that. She had no idea who his father was.

Glancing around the room, his eyes settled on a photograph of her parents, his grandparents. His grandfather had died before Abel was born, but he remembered his grandmother well. Slight like his mother, but warm where she was cold and soft where she was hard. She'd been the one good presence in his early years, and it was the small inheritance that she'd left him which had provided him with his badly needed escape route as soon as he was old enough; money for a one way flight, somewhere as far away from home as he could possibly get.

'I always wanted you to be more like her,' he said, not caring if his words hurt.

If they did, she didn't show it. 'She always wanted me to be more like her. She was a fool. She babied you, and then left me to pick up the pieces.'

'She died, mother.' He couldn't bring himself to use the more familiar 'Mum' any more. 'I don't think she did it to inconvenience you.'

'Yes, and left me to toughen you up for the real world.' She looked him up and down. 'Didn't do a bad job, did I?'

'Anything I am today is in spite of you, not because of you,' he said coldly. It came as a release to let go of any lingering childhood hopes of a good relationship with his mother. In that moment he gave himself permission not to love her any more, and there was no accompanying sensation of loss or grief. There was only relief.

'Well it certainly wasn't your father's influence, was it? None of my men *friends*…' she placed a heavy, sarcastic emphasis on the word '… ever gave you a second look. That's how much you mean to anyone, so quit looking for something that isn't there.'

They stared at each brutally across the chipped table. Abel could see the pleasure in her eyes at having denied him something that he wanted.

If the man who was his father had had even had an inkling about him and never bothered to keep in touch, then he was even less of a loss than his mother. Abel reached inside his jacket and pulled out a folded sheet of paper with the theatre's address on it.

'This is where I'm staying for the next few weeks, if any particular name should come back to you.' He knew now that it wouldn't, but still he dropped the paper on the table before he strode out of the house, down the cracked path and away from it all, forcing himself to walk slowly even though his heart was banging and he wanted to run away, slinking through the shadows just as he had as a boy. He walked. And he walked, and he walked, soaked to the skin, hoping the rain would wash away the smell of his mother's house from his clothes and the look in her eyes from his memory.

He walked to the cemetery and sat on the wet grass with his back leaned against his grandmother's gravestone until after dark, and then he walked into a bar and nursed a double scotch until the bartender locked up for the night. And then he walked the streets some more, drenched by the rain and accompanied by a soundtrack of rolling thunder, and finally headed for the only place that felt anything close to home right now. Theatre Divine.

Chapter Fifteen

Post-show, the packed theatre had emptied out onto the stormy street and all of the staff had hurried home to get out of the worst of the weather, leaving Genie alone on the stage. Tonight's show had been a sizzler. She couldn't hide how excited she was about the future and had thrown all of that euphoric, pent up energy into her act tonight, leaving the audience stamping their feet for more even after her encore. Still mostly in costume, she hummed along to her favourite chill-out playlist streaming through the practice amp offstage as she ran through her post show checks of the lamp to keep her beloved prop in tip top condition.

'Bad luck, showgirl. Looks like your audience lost interest and went home.'

She stilled at the sound of Abel's voice and pirouetted slowly on her high heels. He'd been missing all day; she knew because she'd tried on several occasions to get hold of him and share the happy news about Dalton Productions. Or rub salt into his wounds. One or the other.

Christ. Had he not heard of an umbrella? He was soaked.

'And it looks like you've spent too much time in the sun and forgotten about the English weather,' she observed.

'I wish I'd forgotten a whole lot more about this country than the fucking weather,' he replied, pushing his wet hair back from his eyes.

Did he always have to be so outright antagonistic? She was

on an absolute high and he wasn't going to pull her down.

'Where have you been all day? I've been looking for you,' she said, walking around the lamp again, stretching up high to inspect its upper planes.

He walked slowly down the central aisle, coming closer to her. 'Walking. Thinking about ripping this place apart and starting again.'

Genie smiled inwardly. He'd have to rethink that that one pretty rapidly once he heard her news. 'I see.'

'Do you?' he said, making her turn her head at the sharpness in his voice. 'Do you really? You see why I want turn this place from a washed up gin palace for perverts into a clean, working gym?'

She looked down at him, one hand on the lamp. She'd had just about as much as she could take of his crap about her career.

'Drop it, Kingdom. You find it as sexy as every other audience member. I saw you, remember? You can lie to yourself if you like but you're not fooling me or anyone else. You like to watch me perform.'

He shook his head. 'You don't know how wrong you are, Beauty.' he said softly. 'It disgusts me.'

His harsh choice of words enraged her.

'Disgusts you?' He'd well and truly trampled on her excitement, leaving her ready to kill him. She was no match for him physically, but she was a woman with weapons of her own. There was more than one way to take this man down.

'How about you prove it?' she said, her hand balanced on her tipped up hip.

'I don't need to prove anything to you or anyone else,' he said, with a bitter half laugh.

Genie nodded in acknowledgement, and then walked into the wings and knocked down the house lights apart from a couple of stage spotlights. She returned a moment later with a spindle-backed chair, one of The Divine Girls' stage props. Positioning it carefully on the stage facing the lamp, she turned back to him and opened her hands towards the chair.

'Take a seat. Let me dance for you.'

Abel locked eyes with her. 'I know what you're doing and its not going to work.'

She shrugged delicately. 'So prove me wrong. I dance. You watch. I'm willing to bet you won't be Mr Disgusted of Australia by the end of it.'

'I'm not a gambling man, Genie,' he said, shrugging out of his wet leather jacket to reveal a dark, just as damp shirt that clung to his body and outlined his powerful frame.

'Not even for a sure bet?' She lifted her eyebrows at him and ran her hands down her body to check her costume was in place. 'You're so certain of yourself. What have you got to lose?' she wheedled, moving behind the lamp and using the hidden step to move up onto its lid. He watched her every move from his front row position.

'Come up here and watch me, Abel. What are you so afraid of?'

Under usual circumstances, Abel wasn't an easily persuaded man. Under usual circumstances, he had an iron will.

But this wasn't a usual kind of night, and therefore usual rules didn't apply. His day had been hell on wheels. He'd possibly seen his mother for the last time ever, faced the fact that he'd never meet his father, and he was saturated to the skin. One double whisky hadn't even begun to take the rough edges off his day. He could drink a whole damn bottle and still not feel soothed. And then there was Genie, pushing all of his buttons on purpose in order to prove her fucking point. He badly needed one win today. Everything else had gone to hell; he was ready to sit on that goddamn chair and all but go to sleep while she did her stuff, just to prove for once and for all that he'd rather watch a woman strip paint than strip her clothes off for money. She was taunting him, and he knew that the right thing to do was to walk on by and go to bed, especially in the dark frame of mind that he'd arrived at.

'Not brave enough?' she said softly, and for a split second in his head it wasn't Genie speaking. It was his mother, and he was a child again, and this was going to be that one time when he stood up and said yes, I *am* brave enough. You can't break me.

And with that, he stalked up the stairs at the side of the stage and dropped onto the chair, legs splayed and arms folded across his chest.

'Go for your life, Beauty. Give it your best shot.'

Genie didn't know what had made him change his mind, but she sensed the moment that he snapped. He'd given off an aura of pent up frustration from the second he'd walked in, and now he'd taken his seat she could practically feel it radiating from him like a physical entity. It surrounded her.

She'd never performed for an audience of one before. It brought a new intimacy, a whole different aspect to her act that she hadn't considered hitherto. She was generally so blinded by the stage lights that she couldn't pick out faces in the crowd, but Abel was close enough for her to really be able to see him, to watch his expressions.

She'd positioned his chair beneath a spotlight, and from here she could see the way his damp shirt pulled taut across his chest muscles, and the droplets of rain that still spiked his dark eyelashes like mascara. He was a big man in every sense: tall and robust with a presence to match. There was a quiet, brooding charisma about him tonight, a tight intensity, and Genie found herself more nervous than she expected to be. She'd engineered this situation, and now she had to see it through.

Abel didn't want to look her in the eyes. He could get through this as long as he didn't see the real woman behind the dancing girl she was so intent on making him want. What he didn't want was to see the pretty girl in cut offs and a t-shirt, or the almost virginal one in a white lace nightdress, or the one whose body he'd licked melted chocolate off. He didn't want to connect with her at all, and he figured that as long as he didn't look her in the eyes then he'd be okay. Then she threw her head back and struck a pose, her red curls wild over her shoulders, and he gave up on any plan and just watched her dance.

Genie knew she needed to do something different if this was going to work. He'd seen her current routine on several occasions, and she wanted the element of surprise. Besides, she'd removed her nipple covers after the show and hadn't bothered to put her stockings back on either, so had only the corset and knickers she'd finished her encore in now covering her body.

It wasn't much to work with, but it was going to have to be enough. Closing her eyes, she listened to the current playlist track, finding her rhythm, letting her body undulate to the steady, pulsing beat. Its sultry dance sound wasn't anywhere near as loud as her show music, but it was just enough to give her something to follow.

Rippling her hands down her body, she toyed with the corset catches, watching the spotlit man in front of her. He clearly wanted to give the impression he didn't want to be there. His folded arms, his set jaw, his indifferent expression all said 'bored'. But his eyes didn't as he watched her fingers play with those hook and eye fastenings. However hard Abel tried not to be, she could see he was interested.

He shifted in his seat now, becoming more agitated, and she bypassed her corset to hook her thumbs into the sides of her frilly silk knickers. She saw him swallow, noticing the way he closed his eyes momentarily as he did it. She was so very aware of him, of his proximity, and of his potential to combust. She just didn't know how long his fuse was.

There was only one way to find out. She lifted one eyebrow and smiled a little, suggestive, then slid the knickers down her thighs to reveal the tiny crystal g-string that covered her modesty on stage.

Look me in the eyes, Abel Kingdom.

He looked everywhere else, but he steadfastly refused to meet her gaze. She danced just for him, and every single second she longed for him to look up. It was as if he'd only half accepted her challenge, and given the fact that she was the one who'd thrown the dice, she certainly wasn't prepared to play by his rules.

Leaving her corset in place for now, she struck a new pose, slithering her body over the lamp's jewelled paintwork. It was time to take it up a level.

Fuck. This wasn't her usual act. He'd banked on knowing what came next so he could mentally prepare himself, and now she'd gone a step ahead of him and mixed things up. Abel couldn't help but connect with the way her body moved; she was at one with the music, mermaid-like, her lamp a rock in the ocean as she perched on it and beckoned him to come over and break himself against it. He didn't. *He wouldn't.* Thank God she'd had that g-string on. She'd nearly stopped his fucking heart. And then she nearly stopped it again, because she was sliding her glittering body down from the lamp and coming straight for him.

Genie's heart was beating unnaturally fast as she drew closer to him. She'd never danced like this for anyone, and in climbing down and stepping closer she'd crossed the line from showgirl to something else, something closer to all of the accusations he regularly threw at her. She knew that she was breaking the rules, but Abel wasn't a man who played fair anyway. He played dirty, and right now this was starting to feel pretty dirty too, in a sexy way.

She wasn't sure who held the upper hand. It ought to be her, and yet with every passing second of his passivity, Abel somehow seemed to gain ground.

Making a snap decision, Genie kicked the heat up from sultry private dancer to erotic sex kitten. She slid her fingers down inside the front of her g-string. Abel looked down, unable to resist tracking the movement of her hands, and then, at last, agonisingly slowly, he looked up and met her eyes.

If she'd ever felt sexier in her life, Genie couldn't remember when. His eyes smouldered, daring her to take it further, even though he still didn't move a single goddamn muscle.

Abel could barely breathe. She moved with the grace of a ballet dancer, and she had the lush curves of a vintage Hollywood starlet. She had him utterly enthralled, under her spell, and then when she slid her fingers inside that tiny g-string, his hands physically hurt from resisting the urge to take over the job for her. *I will not touch her. I will not touch her. I will not touch her.* If he told himself enough times he'd believe it. Dragging his gaze up the length of her sparkling, corset-clad body, he made his crucial tactical mistake; he looked into her eyes.

Her excitement mirrored his and pushed it up tenfold. Watching her mouth, her pink lips parted slightly as she touched herself. *I will not kiss her. I will not kiss her. I will not kiss her.* But he wanted to, and he hated himself more than ever for letting the thoughts bleed into his consciousness. *I want to fuck her. I want to fuck her. I fucking want her.*

And then she pushed his resolve frighteningly close to breaking point. She shimmied that g-string down her legs and dropped it in his lap.

Genie couldn't believe she'd done it, and in the same breath she'd known all along that she was going to. Turning away from him as she danced, she bent from the waist and smoothed her hands up the length of her leg from ankle to hip, arching backward as she straightened so her hair brushed over his lap. She pirouetted on her heels to face him as she stood, and moved her hands between her slightly parted legs. Jesus, it was sexy being almost naked and dancing for him like this. His cock clearly hadn't received the memo from his brain about not enjoying her performance; he was rock solid inside his jeans and they both knew it. She was desperate to move in and free him, but that wasn't the game. Abel had to be the one to break.

Moving behind his chair, she placed her hand on the back of it, a fingertip away from touching him. Putting her other hand between her legs, she dipped until her mouth was close to his ear.

'I'm touching myself and imagining that it's you,' she whispered. Abel closed his eyes, his expression almost painful. He was so, so close to cracking. Genie moved around him, naked from the waist down, and with a lithe arch of her leg, she straddled herself over his thighs.

She was beside him, behind him, all around him, touching herself and wanting him, and Abel could feel her dragging his resolve out of his body with her bare hands. He'd never battled harder to keep control of himself, and at the point when she swung her creamy, perfect thigh over his and straddled him, she finally smashed his resolve with a sledgehammer blow. He was barely aware of the animal noise that left his body, and he wasn't in control of his hands when they reached for her and dragged her down hard onto his lap.

The moment he touched her, Genie's body caught fire. She was gasping for him, loving the rough, raw way he smashed his mouth down onto hers, the almost painful pressure of his jeans between her legs. He wasn't gentle, and she didn't want him to be.

'Is this what you want from me, Beauty?' he said, his words thick in his throat. 'Is it?'

His chest heaved under hers, and she all but ripped his shirt from his body to get her hands on him. He shook it off and in one easy movement he stood with her in his arms and backed her up against the lamp. His body shone in the lights, glittered from touching her, and his dark eyes were full of danger as he set her on her feet and trapped her in place with his hips. She'd never seen him like this, so out of control, all of that simmering anger and frustration coming out in his taut movements. He slid a hand between her legs and kissed her hard, his other hand clamping her jaw.

He'd asked her a few seconds back if this was what she wanted. She'd never wanted anything more. He pulled his head up, breathing harshly.

'Get this fucking thing off,' he demanded hoarsely, and a second later he had grasped the top of her corset and yanked it open from top to bottom, leaving her nude. He bent his head and kissed her breasts, hungry, and she buried her hands in his hair and pulled his mouth back up to hers.

'Better?' she whispered, knowing from his moan that it was. His hands were on her breasts, his knee between hers. 'I like being stripped by you.' The dynamic of their sex was hard to fathom; he was physically in charge, and yet she sensed she still had control. 'I want you, Abel,' she told him, moved his hand between her legs, gasped when he pushed two fingers inside her without preamble. It didn't hurt; she was drenched. 'I want you to fuck me right here over the lamp.'

Thunder rolled loud outside the theatre as he slammed his fingers into her, and her eyes flew open as he held her body in place with his and opened his eyes. The expression there was so difficult to read. He was turned on, she knew that much, but there was a darkness there, a torment that she didn't understand. He watched her face intently as he slid his fingers out and then all the way back inside her again, making her cry out and arch her back. Genie couldn't breathe with the need to get him naked and on top of her.

'Please, Abel…' she whispered, dragging her teeth over his bottom lip. 'Lift me up and fuck me on top of the lamp.'

She'd won. There was no doubt about it. Abel touched her everywhere, couldn't get enough of her perfect, gleaming showgirl body in his hands. He mouthed her nipples, rubbed her

148

clit, and when she begged him to, he hoisted her up over that fucking lamp and crawled right on up there with her. He wasn't strong enough, she'd beaten him. Crouching over her splayed, goddess body, he unbuttoned his jeans and shoved them off, as frantic as she was to fuck. She spread her legs wider when he was naked and then locked herself around him, claiming her prize. Every inch of her trembling body glittered, she was all sweet curves and filthy heat and wet sex, and as he settled his cock between her legs and thrust himself home, she raked her nails hard enough down his back to draw blood. Animal marks. Victorious.

Genie opened her eyes as Abel's cock filled her body, his heavy weight pressing her against the coolness of the lamp. His hands fisted in her hair, and she'd never forget the look on his face as he looked down at her, the battle between absolute pleasure and absolute anguish clear. He was breathing hard, his chest heaving, and she tipped her hips up, holding him inside her all the way to his base.

'It's good,' she whispered, needing him to know, smoothing his hair back from his sweat damped brow. He didn't move, his eyes still searching her face, frowning, desperate almost.

Come back, Abel. Don't lose your nerve now.

She moved her hands down the slopes and angles of his back, gentle on him now rather than sharp, feeling the marks she'd left on his skin. 'It's so very good,' she repeated, frightened for him, and then she lifted her head and kissed him long and deep, bringing him back from wherever he'd gone. Rocking him inside her, she held his face in one hand and moved the other over the smooth hardness of his ass. She murmured his name as his hips began to move over hers, slow, satisfying thrusts, agonisingly good pressure over her clitoris.

Abel propped himself up on his elbows, stroking his fingertips down her face, reverential.

'I couldn't do it, Beauty,' he said, screwing into her slowly, and the crack in his voice split a crack through Genie's heart. 'I couldn't stop. You're too strong. Too fucking beautiful.'

She breathed deeply and wrapped him close, moving with him, nowhere close to understanding him, yet in another way feeling she knew him better than he knew himself.

'I don't want you to stop,' she said, and gasped into his mouth when he reached between them to stroke his fingers over her clit. The tenderness of the man unbuttoned her until every inch of her ached for him, for the way he kissed her endlessly as he drew the hard, shuddering orgasm out of her body.

Genie cradled his head in her hands, and she felt his tears on her eyelashes even as his hips spasmed into hers, jerking, spilling, finishing what she'd started.

Abel could feel her hands soothing him, her mouth gentle over his temple, even though she didn't know where his emotion had come from. In truth, he didn't understand it either, and the confused mess of lust and hate and love and revulsion inside his head made him recoil from Genie, crawling away to drag his rain damp jeans back on, retreating like a wounded lion.

She sat up, bewildered and beautiful, her body still flushed from their sex, and seconds later she had followed him down onto the stage.

'Abel...' she said beseechingly, her hand warm on his arm. He jerked away from her, dashing his arm over his eyes as he reached for his shirt, but she took it from his hands.

'No. You're not doing this. You're not going to throw your clothes on and walk away again.'

'Give me my goddamn shirt, Genie,' he ground out, his fists clenching on his thighs. He needed to get away from her. She shook her head, and then, infuriatingly, slid the shirt around her own body and fastened a couple of buttons.

'Not until you talk to me.'

He faced her down. 'Keep the shirt. It was expensive. Consider it payment.'

Tears filled her eyes and her mouth trembled as she fought to keep herself in check.

'You bastard,' she said. 'What we just did…' she looked back towards the lamp, and then at him again. 'What we just did deserves more respect than that, Abel. I don't care what you say, or what you think any more.' Her eyes flashed, clear and honest. 'But what just happened there wasn't wrong and you damn well know it.'

He laughed harshly. 'What just happened there? Do you really want to know what just happened there, showgirl?' He moved away from her because he could feel rage tightening his chest. He settled for grabbing hold of the chair, gripping the back so hard that his knuckles popped white against his tanned hands.

'You made me sit on this… fucking… chair…' he banged it down hard on the stage to punctuate his sentence, drawing pleasure from the way she flinched. 'And you flaunted your fucking body in my face until you got what you fucking… well… wanted…'

She stood her ground, glaring at him as he slammed the chair down again. 'You wanted it just as much.'

He held onto the chairback with one hand, scrubbing the other over his jaw and closing his eyes.

'I'm not proud of it,' he said, so quietly that he thought she probably wouldn't hear him over the rain drumming loudly on the roof.

'Well you should be,' she said, stepping closer, her face softening. 'No one's ever made me feel the way you just did.'

'Then you've obviously been fucking the wrong men,' he answered, hating the idea of her with anyone else. 'It wasn't good, or special. It was a fuck, and now it's over and I need a shower.'

Her face told him his words hurt, and he didn't have the vocabulary or the composure to make her understand him in a less painful way. She'd never understand. How could she? How could he tell her of the huge ball of shame and fear that had lived inside him since he'd been a six-year-old kid?

'You need a shower,' she repeated his words back at him, her eyes turning stormy. 'Why, to wash me off your skin?'

To wash her off, and to wash the whole sorry, rancid day off; the encounter with his mother, the truth about his father, the grief for his grandmother.

'What do you want from me, Genie? Lies about how it meant something? Do you expect me to buy you roses and hold your coat while you spend your evenings entertaining as many men as you can fit into your shitty little theatre? Because it's never going to happen.'

He didn't add that he'd already spent too many years of his life waiting for the attention of a woman who'd spent her evenings entertaining as many men as she could muster.

'Don't mock me,' she said, squaring her shoulders.

'Then stop fucking with me,' he shot back. 'Stop trying to prove your fucking point at every chance you get. Stop shoving it down my throat. You win, okay? You. Fucking. Win. You made me do the one thing I swore I wouldn't. What more do you want from me?'

'The one thing?' she said, glaring at him. 'What one thing?'

His blood pounded unnaturally fast around his body. Rationally, he knew Genie wasn't a whore. But emotionally, right down deep inside the darkest part of him, he couldn't keep the distinction clear. She blurred the lines, dancing between showgirl and stripper and hooker, leaving him utterly disorientated, feeling like a kid again. She held the power, down here at least, and he didn't know how to get it back. Besides attacking her with insults and belittling the overwhelming sex they'd just had. He heard his own voice, knew he sounded desperate, unhinged, making no sense. With an effort, he tried to pull himself back.

'Stop it, Genie.'

She heard his quiet warning, and she laughed aloud. 'Stop what?' She threw her hands out to the sides. 'Stop calling you out for lying about what happened here tonight?'

'I'm asking you nicely,' he said, his hands a vice around the chair. 'Go to bed. Please go to bed.'

'You don't get to screw me over my lamp and then dismiss me from my own stage, Abel Kingdom,' she declared, braver than she should have been.

'And you don't get to tell me what to do,' he said, his head swimming with images of her spread out for him on the lamp, and then spread out for everyone else to look at tomorrow. He didn't see the stage costume she wore for everyone else. He saw only her naked curves and her wild red waves, his fantasy tonight and someone else's tomorrow. He saw red, fury, frustration, and he couldn't hold it back any longer.

Lifting the chair above his head, he swung it down hard over the lamp, smashing both the back of the chair and the lid of the glittering prop. Rhinestones scattered the stage, and beside him Genie shouted at him to stop.

Let her shout.

Let her scream.

The blood pounding in his head and the rolling thunder outside drowned her out anyway. He looked at the broken chair in his hands for a second and then brought it down again hard over the back of the lamp, watching as a huge crack opened up down the side of it.

She was yelling, screaming his name, but he didn't stop. He couldn't. The rage burned bright in his chest, and he threw what was left of the chair to the floor and set about wrenching the lamp apart with his bare hands. He was bleeding and still he tore at it, stamped on it with his bare feet, deaf to the sound of her voice and the storm crashing around outside, on and on until all that was left on the bare stage boards was an unrecognisable pile of gilt and crystal encrusted fragments.

Abel stilled, finally done, on his knees, his face wet with sweat and angry tears when he covered it with his blood-streaked hands.

She was still there when he looked up, damp cheeked with her arms wrapped around herself, vulnerable in his too big shirt. Her wide, shocked eyes locked with his, stripping him down to the bare metal. She saw him. Saw everything there was to see laid bare in front of her; the badness, the unlovable boy, the inadequate man. She saw inside him, and still she crossed the stage and knelt amongst the carnage to hold him.

Over the theatre a white bolt of lightning lit up the night sky, and neither of them saw the storm-damaged rafters fall until a split second before the debris tumbled down towards the stage, too late for anything to be done except for Abel to hurl his body over Genie's in a belated, instinctive gesture of protection.

Chapter Sixteen

Genie sat on a front row seat and stared at the same ugly debris again several days later, still barely able to comprehend what had happened. She shouldn't even have been in there. The fire service and building safety inspectors had taken one look at the damage and declared the place unsafe.

The fact that the theatre was a listed building vastly complicated any prospect of repair. And then there was the cost. The roof had already been in need of serious work, and after the storm damage, it now needed replacing entirely. Hundreds of thousands of pounds she didn't have, and never would have now, thanks to the storm. She'd just come off the phone with Ada, who'd regretfully informed her that given their tight filming schedules, Dalton productions had no choice but to withdraw their offer to use the theatre as a movie set and look for somewhere else.

That was that then. No money. No roof. No theatre. No home. No job.

And then in amongst all of that misery, she'd lost Abel Kingdom too.

'Genie?'

She turned at the sound of her uncle's voice, and gave him a small, sad smile as he made his way down the central aisle and came to sit beside her.

'I knew I'd find you here,' he said. 'But sitting staring at it isn't going to help.'

She nodded, her eyes on the stage. 'For a while there I really did think I was going to do it,' she said, reflecting on what might have been. She'd told her uncle everything about Dalton Productions after the storm, and was only glad she hadn't told him before so that he didn't have to feel as gutted as she was.

'I know, G. I'm proud of you for even trying.' He patted her jean-clad knee and sighed heavily. 'Sometimes I think things happen for a reason. Maybe this is the old girl's way of telling us it's time to move on.'

Tears stung her eyes. 'I don't want to,' she said. 'I want to live here again with you, like we used to.'

He put his arm around her shoulders and gave her his handkerchief to wipe her eyes, just as he always had.

'I'd like that too, darling, but look up. Look around. There's a chance the insurance might cover some of it, but they knew it was already in need of work,' he said gently. 'And the time it would take. How long before we could start turning any sort of profit again?' He sighed and looked at her, forcing himself to be honest. 'Besides, it's more than that. It's me. These weeks of living with Robin have shown me that there *is* life outside of here. I'm no spring chicken anymore G.' He squeezed her tight. 'Those high heels are playing hell with my knees these days.'

Genie had sensed his contentment with his new living arrangements, and she knew it was wrong to feel abandoned by the one person who'd never failed her, to begrudge him the happiness that his life with Robin had brought him. It was just that circumstances lately had left her feeling very alone, and the only certainty she had right now was a few weeks on Deanna's uncomfortable couch while she sorted herself out. It wasn't much to go on.

'How's Abel Kingdom doing now?'

Genie focused her attention on knotting her uncle's handkerchief around her fingers.

'All right, I think.'

'You think?'

She glanced up at the damaged roof. 'He's refused to see me.'

And there it was, the most upsetting fact in all of this. She'd been terrified when Abel had been knocked unconscious by the falling debris, scrabbling out from beneath him, inexpertly checking his pulse and finding nothing. She'd found his mobile in his discarded jacket and called an ambulance, sobbing down the phone so hard that the operator could barely make her words out. The hours afterwards had been a blur of anxiety and panic, punctuated by moments of overwhelming relief. He was breathing. He was injured, but at least he was breathing. The ambulance crew seemed concerned about his head and his shoulder, as she sat beside him on the way to the hospital and prayed only that he'd live. She didn't care about the theatre, or her own lesser cuts and bruises. She thought only of him, on his knees seconds before the accident, already a broken man. She berated herself a million times over for the way she'd relentlessly goaded him, pushed him to breaking point to prove herself right. And after all of that, she hadn't proved herself right at all. In breaking Abel, she'd broken herself too. She wasn't fanciful enough to believe that the physical destruction of the theatre had been of her doing too, but it felt like a bitter irony, as if the tempest playing out on the stage had somehow invited in the deadly bolt struck by the storm outside.

'Mr Kingdom, please! You can't leave, the consultant hasn't discharged you.'

Abel looked up, buttoning his shirt with difficulty. 'Send me the paperwork in the mail. I'll sign to say you're not responsible.'

The young nurse rounded the bed. 'It doesn't work like that, I'm afraid. You really need to get back into bed and re…'

Abel's words cut across hers. 'I've spent three days lying in that bed looking out of that window at that godforsaken greyness. I'm done here. My head's fine.' He pulled the bandage from around his skull with his good arm. 'I can see perfectly well, and a fractured shoulder isn't going to stop me from catching my flight home.'

'You can't fly, Mr Kingdom! Please, let me try to get hold of the registrar at least!' She backed out of his room purposefully, and Abel sighed darkly. He was leaving this place today. He'd booked a flight home that left in a few hours' time, and one way or the other, he was going to be on it.

He didn't need to pack. All of his belongings had been at the theatre and none were salvageable. He had the clothes he'd arrived in, his jacket, and his wallet. Along with the emergency passport his PA in Australia had organised a couple of days back, it was going to have to be enough to get him home, because he'd had a skinful of London and everything that went along with it.

Coming back here had been the biggest mistake he'd ever made. He'd thought he could stamp his authority all over the places that had haunted him as a child, and he'd come to realise since the day of the accident that he didn't have the stomach to see it through. London had defined his childhood, it wasn't possible to come back and scrub the bad memories out of existence.

Abel had learned over the years to choose his battles wisely, in most areas of his life. He now knew that however painfully personal this battle was, he couldn't win it. He wasn't peaceful with his decision, but the only alternative was to stay here and risk tearing himself to pieces completely to see it through to its bitter end. That simply wasn't an option. London diminished him. It stole his spirit and infected him with its cold, grey bleakness. He wasn't proud of the man he'd become here and he wasn't going to let the process go any further.

Sighing heavily, he picked up the painkillers from his bedside table and tossed them down his throat. His shoulder hurt like a bitch and his headache was no picnic either. The accident in the theatre had been the last straw. How many more signs did he need before he accepted that this thing just wasn't going to work out? The meeting with his mother shouldn't have hurt, he'd known what to expect, after all. The news about his father too:

on reflection, he'd have been more surprised had his mother have given him any concrete information. It was a hard fact to face that not just one but two parents were utterly indifferent to his existence, but it wouldn't break him. His mother had taught him early on not to believe in fairytales.

But the biggest reason he was leaving was Genie. He'd never known a woman like her before, someone with such clarity about who she was, or such conviction in her beliefs. She was dangerous to him. Toxic. Her obstinate challenges had backed him into a corner, and he'd come out fighting. He couldn't explain it or apologise for it, even though he was deeply ashamed of the way he'd behaved. He didn't want to feel the way she made him feel: insecure and out of control. He only had to look at her and she had him, hook line and sinker, and he didn't trust her not to haul him so far out of the water that he couldn't survive. That was why he was going home.

Because he'd met his match.

Standing stiffly, Abel picked up his jacket and walked out of the hospital ward.

Genie rode the hospital elevator up to Abel's floor, then stood rooted to the spot when the doors slid open and revealed the man himself standing there waiting to ride it back down again.

He reacted the exact same way, then shot her a look that could have killed a less robust person and stepped inside with her.

Oh God, oh God, oh God. What could she say to him? She'd come here today as she had every day since he'd been admitted, but in truth she hadn't expected to actually see him. He'd turned her away each time, nurses at the ward's door politely declining her company on his behalf, though she was pretty sure they weren't passing on his exact words. To find herself granted an audience with him now came as a shock.

'Abel,' she said softly, turning to him. His profile didn't flicker a muscle.

'Don't,' he said.

'Are you leaving?' The ward sister had told her on the phone earlier that they anticipated he'd need to stay in for at least another few days yet. She'd been able to get updates on his progress because she was on record as having brought him in, despite not being family. It was a small victory.

'What's it look like?'

'Abel, please. At least look at me.'

His jaw tightened, but he didn't glance her way. Genie knew full well that her time with him was going to be up in a matter of seconds, and in a panic she turned and pressed the emergency stop button.

Abel looked her way at last, a slow, cold flick of his eyes. 'If you're expecting a repeat performance of the last time we were in a lift together you're going to be disappointed.'

She took his insult and let it hang. 'You don't look well enough to get out of here.'

He didn't; he looked pale, and strained, and he needed a shave.

'A nurse *and* a stripper, huh? There really is no end to your talents, Beauty.'

Another barb. Genie winced, letting him throw his arrows. What she needed to say was too important to get dragged into the argument he was spoiling for.

'Were you going to leave without saying goodbye?'

He turned to her then, revealing his arm strapped across his chest in a dark sling beneath his jacket. 'We're not friends, Genie, and this isn't the movies. I don't think either of us needs an emotional farewell scene.'

Genie felt his detachment all the way to her bones. 'I don't want you to go,' she said, desperate and raw, and he looked at her, completely unreadable.

'Why not? You made your point pretty fucking well, don't you think? We've established the fact that I fuck strippers. What do you want me to do? Get it tattooed across my head so I see it everyday for the rest of my goddamn life?'

Anguish filled Genie's throat with tears. He was too angry to listen to what she needed to say, but he was leaving her life and if she didn't say it now she'd probably never get a second chance.

'I'm sorry, Abel. I'm so, so sorry for what happened the other night.'

'Don't turn on the crocodile tears on my account,' he said, leaning his back against the wall, his face flinching in pain.

'Do you have to keep ramming the point home about how low your opinion is of me?' she said, finally biting. 'Never in my life has anyone constantly belittled me as you have, Abel Kingdom and I hate the fact that that I can't help loving you regardless.'

She stopped speaking several words too late, her chest heaving, both of them shell shocked.

It was the last way she'd wanted to say those words for the first time to the man she'd realised she loved as he'd knelt amongst her smashed up lamp, broken and in tears. In that moment she'd known that somewhere along the line he'd been wounded deeply, that whatever his hang-ups, they weren't really about her. The fact that she'd pushed him into facing them so starkly made her insides twist with regret. She'd sat beside him in the ambulance that night and wondered if she'd ever get to tell him that she loved him.

'You love me?' he said. 'Have you lost your fucking mind?'

It wasn't the ideal response.

'Probably,' she said, aching to hold him and knowing he'd push her away. 'Please don't go. Stay. Take the theatre. It doesn't matter to me as much as you do. Nothing does.'

He stared at her long and hard, like someone trying to understand an abstract piece of art.

'You're on some fucked up kind of guilt trip,' he said, eventually. 'You'll get over it.' He gestured at his shoulder. 'So will I.'

'You're right, Abel, I do feel guilty. I pushed you and I shouldn't have made you do something I knew you didn't want to.'

He half laughed. 'It was sex, Genie. Fucking. You didn't make me do it. I did it because I'd had the day from hell and I thought it might make me feel better. It didn't. Quit blaming yourself and get on with your life.'

'Really?' she said, rounding on him. 'Really? As simple as that? I tell you I love you, and you tell me to get over it then jump on a plane to the other side of the world?'

He nodded. 'It's every bit as simple as that. You can keep your tears, and your pathetic excuse for a theatre. I want none of it.'

Wow. He was hard, but she knew better. 'I don't believe this anti-love, tough guy act. I've seen you, remember? I've seen behind your smoke and mirrors, Abel.'

That registered. He glared at her. 'That's exactly my fucking point,' he shot back, his dark eyes furious. 'I don't want smoke and mirrors, or lies, or to feel this shitty.' The bleak dejection on his face sliced her heart in half. 'That's exactly why I'm going to fly half way around the world to get away. I can't think straight,' he said, getting closer to the truth now, in spite of himself. The anger left his voice, leaving behind a hollow sadness. 'I can't breathe around you.'

Was this how it was going to end? A painful conversation in a crappy hospital elevator? Genie couldn't have imagined a more unsatisfactory fairytale.

'So go,' she said wretchedly. 'Go back home to your beloved big skies, and breathe it all in deep. Fill your lungs, Abel, but I promise you it won't make you as happy as I can, if you'll let me. I know you better now.' She moved close to him and touched his arm, almost crying at the familiar scent of him. She ached for him to hold her. 'I love you.'

He looked down at her, and she up at him, and the connection that had been there from the first moment they'd met was as strong as ever.

'I'm not anti-love, Genie,' he said, as the lift jolted into life. 'I'm just anti-loving you.'

Genie leaned against the wall and wrapped her arms around herself to hold the pain in as she watched him walk away, taking her heart with him back to the flip side of the world. He didn't look back.

Chapter Seventeen

If Genie had imagined that Abel would go home and then realise he'd made a huge mistake and come back for her, she would have been disappointed. Days dragged into weeks, and the first and last thing she did every day was to check her emails and texts, with her heart in her mouth in case his name was there. It wasn't.

Life on Deanna's sofa was an endless round of late night glasses of wine and heart to hearts, but they could do little to ease Genie's distress. She'd fallen fast, hard and completely for Abel; he'd rolled into her life and taken over it from the first moment she'd laid eyes on him.

She'd always imaged falling in love would be about romantic candlelit dinners and picnics in the park, a gradual build up to a grand passion, not a rush of white hot lust and emotion that would leave her reeling and trying to stay standing up. He'd blown her away from the second he'd had her write her number on his arm, and she missed his presence in her life more than she knew how to put into words.

The theatre paled into a poor second. She was almost glad not to have to get up on stage, she wasn't sure her body would have been capable of conning an audience into believing she was having a good time up there. Ever since he'd arrived, she knew now that she'd danced only for him in her head. Had she have been more watchful of her own emotions, she'd have seen the signs, but she'd been so wrapped up in battling him that she hadn't noticed herself falling. She'd fallen all the same, and she'd let herself get so badly injured that she wasn't sure how in hell's name to mend herself.

The doctor couldn't cure her. Deanna couldn't cure her. Genie couldn't cure herself. She was hopelessly in love with a man who didn't love her back, one who'd deliberately moved himself as far away around the globe as he could to be away from her. It was a pretty categorical rebuff.

Abel buried himself in work. He'd been a fool to ever go back to London: he'd come home feeling ashamed, with his tail between his legs, bashed, beaten and worse off in every possible way. His shoulder hurt like hell in the weeks immediately after his return, but he welcomed the physical pain because it went some way towards blocking out the other worse stuff.

He hadn't expected to spare any more thoughts for his mother, yet she still weighed heavily on his mind. Somewhere deep inside he'd harboured childish hopes that there was more to their relationship than apathy and bad memories, but the plain truth was that there wasn't. There just wasn't. He'd lost his mother in London as surely as if he'd stood at her graveside and thrown in a handful of earth, and she'd taken any answers about his father to that metaphorical grave with her too. Abel struggled on, orphaned by circumstance, alone by choice.

He didn't think of Genie at all. No way.

He didn't think of her in the shower in the mornings as he tried to scrub her from beneath his skin.

He didn't think of her as he ran on the beach, trying to pound all thoughts of her into the sand.

He didn't think of her at night when he chased her out of his dreams and woke clammy all over, reaching across the cold, empty sheets. He saw her time and time again as she'd been just before the ceiling came down, coltish in his oversized shirt, stunned by his rage. Shame dirtied him, and if he'd stayed it would have dirtied her too.

How long would this go on for? It had been eight weeks,

and already it felt like eight years. His arm had now mostly healed thanks to diligent exercise and the best physiotherapy that money could buy, yet inside he was still every bit as fucked up as the day he'd flown home. His head was a mess, and whichever way he looked at it, he couldn't see a way out of this besides to keep getting up every morning, hoping it wouldn't hurt quite as much.

In five days the theatre would be repossessed. Genie had been mentally crossing the days off in her head with a big black marker, like a captive etching marks into the wall of their prison cell. There was nothing to be done but wait, so she just let the days wash over her one by one. She was ready to drown. What use was the theatre now? So much had changed. Her uncle had moved onto the next stage of his life, happily sliding into a disreputable retirement with Robin. She couldn't imagine herself ever performing again either: her limbs were heavy, her body didn't want to move to music and her skin was as grey as the London skyline.

She knew that she'd gone as low as she could physically and mentally go, and as hard as it was going to be, in five days time she was going to hand over the keys to this place and draw a line in the sand. Her uncle had raised her well. He'd taught her optimism, and pride, and to walk through life with her glass half full. She'd let it run dangerously close to empty. Five days, and then no more.

She ran her hand over the dusty reception desk, remembering her first encounter with Abel right there on that spot. He'd been so cocky, and she had been so intent on finding out what he wanted that she didn't take the time to really look at him. Sure, she'd noticed he was hot, but she should have seen more, should have taken the time to notice the vulnerable man behind the facade. Because no one was really what they seemed at face value, were they? Everyone has more to them if you bother to look, and she'd bothered to look to late.

A tap on the locked glass doors made her frown and look

up. Wasn't it obvious that the place was closed? Was the scaffolding not enough of a sign that things were deeply amiss in here? Genie was flouting every safety rule in the book by being here herself, yet she was drawn back day after day, to keep the old girl company, holding a bedside vigil for a beloved.

Outside, a girl was huddled against the glass, her hair as dark as the goth circles drawn around her eyes. Genie sighed, knowing she was going to have to go and be polite because she'd now made the mistake of making eye contact.

Unlocking the door, she pushed it open.

'We're not looking for dancers I'm afraid,' she said, barely looking at the girl. 'We're closed.'

The girl dragged her thin jacket around her skinny body. 'I'm not a dancer,' she mumbled, thrusting a scrap of paper at Genie, leaving her no choice but to take it. 'I'm looking for him.'

Unfolding the paper, Genie looked down, reading the rounded, childish handwriting slowly.

Abel Kingdom. Theatre Divine.

She folded the paper back up with a terse shake of her head. 'He isn't here.'

A hesitant flicker of uncertainty passed through the girl's heavily kohled eyes. 'So when's he coming back?'

Genie half laughed, half sighed, wrapping her arms around her torso. 'He isn't.'

The girl's eyebrows knitted together. 'Never?'

It was as if she were speaking the word Genie hadn't dared to. She shook her head, her eyes looking past the slight frame of the stranger and back over the weeks when she'd had him here and missed every chance she'd had to create anything other than conflict.

'I don't think he is, no.'

The girl's shoulders slumped. 'Do you know where he's gone?'

'Home.' Genie said. 'He's gone back to Australia.'

'No!' the girl exclaimed, unguarded and alarmed, and her

tone of voice finally pulled Genie from her self-indulgent state. Looking at her visitor properly for the first time, Genie realised her mistake. Despite the heavy make-up, this girl couldn't be more than sixteen years old. Younger, possibly. As Genie watched her carefully she pulled herself together, shoving her chin in the air with an air of shabby defiance.

'Right,' she said, snatching the folded paper back from Genie's fingers and shoving it into the pocket of her sprayed on jeans. 'Figures.' She hesitated for a moment as if she was going to say something further, then turned and walked back down the steps.

Genie watched her slender body move away, and on impulse followed her and placed a hand on her shoulder. Many years ago she herself had been abandoned on these steps. She wouldn't turn her back on someone else in trouble now.

'Who are you?'

The girl turned back and shrugged. 'I don't know.' She stared for a second and then turned away again. Genie was faster this time, stepping around her onto the pavement.

'I'm sorry I was sharp,' she said. 'Please. If you're looking for Abel I can probably help you.' She didn't miss the badly disguised flare of hope in the girl's brown eyes. 'Come back inside. We can talk easier in there.'

'Shit,' the girl said, wide-eyed, as she looked at the state of the place. Genie gestured for her to take a seat in the back row of the stalls. 'It looks like someone dropped a bomb on the stage.'

It was as apt a description as any. Genie certainly felt as if someone had dropped a grenade right into the middle of her life and pulled out the pin. Sitting down alongside her visitor, she crossed her legs and studied her.

'So. Let's start again. I'm Genie Divine,' she said. 'This is my family's theatre.' She didn't add that it wouldn't be by this time next week.

The girl's eyes darted around, taking in the beauty and the

damage that surrounded them.

When she finally looked back at Genie, it was to reply, tentatively. 'I'm Lizzie. Lizzie Kingdom.'

Genie looked at her, and then stared at her. 'Kingdom?' she said, slowly, as if it were another language.

The girl, Lizzie, nodded.

'Are you related to Abel?' Genie asked, trying to fathom the link.

One of Lizzie's delicate shoulders lifted as she huffed out. 'Apparently.'

This wasn't making any sense. 'You might have to help me out here, Lizzie. I don't get it.'

Lizzie shook her head and her slender fingers played with the hem of her faded tee shirt. 'I don't either, really.'

The jaded tone of her voice struck Genie as odd for someone barely more than a child. Even though she'd known Lizzie for all of ten minutes, the urge to wrap her arms around her came from nowhere. She didn't though; she just sat and waited for her to speak again.

'I think he's my brother.'

'Oh,' Genie said, winded. Thinking back to their lunch date upstairs, Genie was certain he had told her he had no siblings. Had he lied? 'Does he… does he know about you?'

Lizzie looked down, hiding her eyes. 'Dunno.'

It was like trying to do a jigsaw with a blindfold on. Genie tried another tack. 'How old are you, Lizzie?'

'Fourteen.' Lizzie looked up again, her expression guarded. 'Why?'

Genie shook her head, still confused. 'And you've never met Abel?'

'I'd never even heard of him until a couple of days ago.'

Okay. 'So who told you?'

There it was again, that jaded, hunted look. 'My mother.' She paused. 'Our mother.'

'Your mother told you out of the blue that you have a

brother you've never even met?'

'Well, she didn't exactly tell me.' Lizzie rolled her eyes. 'I found his name and address on a piece of paper in the kitchen bin yesterday. 'She grabbed it off me and ripped it up when I asked her about it, yelling and all that.' Lizzie's mouth turned down in distaste. 'Didn't matter. I remembered what it said and wrote it down again.'

Genie sat quietly, listening to Lizzie and trying to work out how Abel could not even know his sister existed.

'Do you live with your mum, Lizzie?'

Lizzie snorted and looked away. 'Sometimes.'

How could a young girl, a child really, live anywhere *sometimes*? She waited silently for Lizzie to elaborate.

'I lived there when I was a kid,' she said.

Genie nodded, a little heartbroken already for this tough little girl. Because she *was* little. She was still a kid.

'Then the social got involved, and I lived a whole load of other places too. Sometimes back with her. Sometimes not.' Lizzie shrugged. 'Doesn't matter. I'm old enough to look after myself now.'

She so obviously wasn't that Genie wanted to wrap her in a blanket and give her hot chocolate.

'And the first you knew of Abel was this piece of paper?'

Lizzie nodded. 'I asked her who it was. Because of the surname, see? She did some more yelling and said he'd called round out of the blue weeks ago, flashing his cash and laughing at us.'

It didn't sound at all like the Abel Genie knew. 'I'm not sure he even knows you exist, Lizzie,' she said, carefully.

'Probably won't care,' Lizzie said, full of false bravado.

Genie couldn't offer Lizzie any guarantees, but everything inside her told her that Abel didn't know that this child had even been born. It made sense. He'd left at eighteen. His mother could have had another child, if she'd had him at a relatively young age, and by the sounds of it, he hadn't been home since. The dark parts of him that she hadn't understood were slowly starting to become clearer. He'd had the same start in life as the girl beside her, and looking at her now, there were obvious similarities. Lizzie shared Abel's dark, expressive eyes, and the same full mouth. Realising those things made it almost hard to look at her.

'You remind me of him,' she said softly, without thinking.

'Do I?'

Genie nodded. 'Yes.'

'Are you his girlfriend?'

The ghost of a smile touched Genie's lips at the idea of being Abel's girlfriend. It seemed too childish a term to apply to the feelings she had for him.

'No,' she said in the end. 'But I do know him pretty well.'

Did she? In some ways maybe, and yet she'd learned things about him today that had subtly painted him more clearly in her mind. She knew the man he was, but she still had much to learn about the child he'd been.

'Will you let me email him for you?' she asked, trying to work out how best to help both Lizzie and Abel. She had his email address from business messages her uncle had forwarded. She didn't let herself feel anything for herself; this wasn't about her.

'All right.' Lizzie shrugged, aiming for casual and not managing it as well as she must have hoped. She added, in a rush, 'Shall I come back again another day?'

Genie watched the girl gather herself together to leave. 'Where are you sleeping tonight, Lizzie?'

Lizzie's mouth twisted with sarcasm. 'Home. She *works* on Tuesday nights, thank God.' Lizzie drew air quotes around the word 'work' as she spoke.

Genie nodded, walking Lizzie to the door. Lizzie's tone set off a whole series of alarm bells. 'What does your mother do?' she ventured, every bit as fake casual as Lizzie had been earlier.

'She likes to say she's a hostess.' Lizzie laughed, a thin, miserable sound that said she thought it anything but funny.

Genie didn't push any further. She'd heard enough to draw

her own conclusions, and her heart twisted for the man on the other side of the world. Reaching out, she laid a hand on Lizzie's shoulder.

'Come back and see me again tomorrow?'

Lizzie hesitated, then nodded and hurried quickly down the steps and away.

It turned out to be a difficult email to write. Genie pressed delete more times than she could count, trying to keep her own emotions out of her words. She so wanted to ask him to come back for her. She typed out how very much she loved him and then deleted it. She told him instead of the girl she'd met that afternoon; how Lizzie shared Abel's eyes, the scant details she'd revealed of her home life.

How should she end the email? Love Genie? Regards, Genie? In the end she simply signed it G, her heart in her mouth as her finger hovered over the send button before she pressed it, breathing out hard when it was done. Glancing at the clock in the corner of her screen, Genie calculated it would be the early hours of the morning now for Abel. She didn't need to check out the time difference. She knew it by heart.

Closing her emails, she locked the theatre doors and headed for Deanna's flat, which passed for home just now.

Huddled inside her coat at the bus stop ten minutes later, her phone buzzed. Pulling it out, her email alert flashed. One new message. Clicking her inbox, Genie's heart jumped involuntarily at the sight of his name. She'd longed so often to see it there, and now there it was.

The bus came, and people moved around her to board it while she stayed rooted to the spot, staring at the screen. She didn't notice the driver duck to try to catch her eye, or see him close the doors with a shrug before he pulled away.

She clicked on the message, desperate for news of him. There was just one line of text. Five words. No greeting, no sign off.

I'm on the next plane.

Chapter Eighteen

'You sure you don't want me to come in with you?' Deanna asked, protectively.

Genie shook her head, glancing into the window of the cafe a few doors down from the theatre. It was quiet in there, too late for breakfast, too early for lunch.

'I need to do this on my own, Dee.'

Deanna nodded. 'I'm a call away if you need me,' she said, leaning in and hugging her friend. 'Be careful around him, okay?'

Genie hugged Deanna to her carefully to avoid squashing the ever-present camera around her neck. 'I will.' They'd spent enough late nights talking over what went wrong, for Deanna to be more than aware of how much power Abel had over Genie right now.

'Go. You'll be late for class.' She pushed her friend gently off down the road with a small, affectionate smile, then turned and headed into the warmth of the cafe.

She was early, deliberately so, to give herself chance to gather herself together. It had been two days since Abel's message. She knew from the second, equally scant email she'd received from him that he'd landed at Heathrow last night and checked into a hotel. He had made arrangements in the briefest of words to meet her here today at noon. Lizzie was going to join them half an hour later. She'd spent the afternoon at the theatre yesterday, and from the snippets she'd revealed of her home life, Genie was painfully aware of how difficult an existence she'd had up to now.

Lizzie hadn't been able to hide her shock when Genie had told her that Abel was flying over. Any doubts about whether he'd known about her and disregarded her were chased away instantly as childish hope lit her face.

'Wow,' she'd said. 'That's fast.'

'He's kind of like that,' Genie had observed.

Lizzie had fallen silent for a while, chewing her lip. 'What if he doesn't like me?'

Genie had rolled her eyes and squeezed the younger girl impulsively around the shoulders. 'He will,' she'd said. 'Trust me. He will.'

Sitting in the cafe nursing a mug of coffee between her palms, Genie watched the windows for him. She was nervous, the kind of gut wrenching nervous that makes you breathless and on the edge of panic. She didn't doubt he'd come. He was coming for Lizzie's sake, but that made it even more difficult to read the situation. How would he be with Genie when he came in? Openly hostile? Distantly polite? She wouldn't know how to handle either. It would have to be enough just to see him, what came next was up to him.

Her throat constricted as she caught sight of the tall, familiar figure crossing the road between the traffic, and her hands trembled a little around the mug. *He was here.*

She watched as he scanned the cafe, and held her breath when his eyes met hers. He didn't smile, just studied her for a long second before threading his way through the tables to get to her. Relief overwhelmed her at the sight of him; it was almost painfully good to look at him again. He pulled the chair opposite hers out and sat down.

They faced each other wordlessly across the table, and tears rushed into her eyes. She just loved him so damn much.

'You look well,' she managed, nodding towards his unstrapped shoulder.

He nodded. 'I am.'

She looked down when he spoke, letting the sound of his voice soak into her bones. She wanted to remember the sound of him forever. When she looked up again he was studying her.

'How've you been?' he asked.

She half smiled, half shrugged. 'All right. You know.'

He looked up at the waitress as she hovered nearby and asked for a couple of fresh coffees.

'And the theatre?' he said. He must have seen the state of it as he'd walked past.

'Gone. Or else it will have in a few days.' She sighed heavily. 'Probably for the best.'

If he was surprised, he didn't show it. They fell into silence as the waitress placed two steaming mugs in front of them and whisked Genie's old one away.

'How is she?' he asked. 'How's Lizzie?' There was already affection and anxiety in the way he said her name.

Genie smiled at the thought of Lizzie. 'She's a sweet kid.'

His expression darkened. 'I should have been here.'

It was so like him to take the guilt onto his own shoulders. 'How could you have been? You didn't even know she existed.'

His mouth thinned into a line. 'I was so intent on getting away. Always running. If I'd known...' he huffed out and dragged his mug towards him.

'You didn't know, Abel. Don't blame yourself. This wasn't your mistake, and you're here now. That's what matters.'

He didn't look convinced. 'Fourteen fucking years. Why didn't my mother ever tell me? I came back once in that time and she never said a word. I would have stayed if I'd known. Knowing that she... what she...' He looked down, unable to finish his sentence.

'Don't do this. Don't go over and over what might have been. It won't help either of you.'

Genie spoke from experience, but wasn't great at taking her own advice. From the day Abel had left she'd gone over and over what she could have said or done to make him stay. She'd become an expert at wishful thinking, hurting herself with perfect daydreams of what might have been if only she'd played things differently.

She raised her gaze and held his.

'We should talk,' he said, quietly. 'Not right now, but I won't leave without coming to find you first.'

Genie nodded, tears tightening her throat again until she didn't trust herself to speak. Just knowing that he wasn't going to run out of her life again without a chance at least to talk was enough to overwhelm her.

'Don't,' he said, reaching across the table and covering her hands with his around her mug. 'I can't watch you cry again.'

She couldn't help herself. She couldn't look at him; he stole her breath. Beneath the table his knee brushed her leg, and his hands were warm and strong over hers. She wanted to stop the world turning and stay there forever with him in that small, steamy cafe.

'Genie?' An uncertain voice spoke her name, and when she looked up, Lizzie was hovering behind Abel, looking smaller than ever in the shadow of her brother's powerful frame. Abel pulled his arms sharply back across the table and Genie jumped to her feet, dashing the backs of her hands over her eyes.

'Lizzie, you're here!' she said, hugging her quickly as Abel stood and turned around.

Lizzie kept hold of Genie's hand as she looked up at her big brother for the first time. 'Abel?' she said, tentative and awkward.

He nodded, silently taking her in.

'Lizzie was our nanna's name,' he said gently, and then he pulled his little sister into a hug and held her to him tightly.

Genie stepped back, choked with emotion for them and for herself. She reached for her jacket and walked out of the cafe, knowing that Abel and Lizzie could take it from here.

Genie sat on the foyer floor with her back resting against the theatre's welcome desk, her fingers tracing the intricate pattern of the floor tiles. It was so familiar to her that she could have drawn it with her eyes closed.

She watched people rush past the steps outside the glass doors in search of their lunch and wondered how things were going further on down the road in the cafe. She didn't doubt Abel; she knew that she'd passed Lizzie into safe hands.

Wrapping her arms around her knees, she laid her head on them and closed her eyes, trying to commit every micro detail of him to her memory forever. The clean, warm scent of him, his reassuringly powerful presence, the curve of his cheek. She'd wanted so much for him to walk in and pull her into those strong arms of his, to love her as much as she loved him, a scene from a cheesy Valentine movie come to life. She caught herself, gave herself a mental shake. When did she get so pathetic? He'd promised not to leave before they had the chance to talk. It was something. Maybe, just maybe, if she said the exact right things, she had a chance. She just wished she knew what the right things were.

A knock on the glass made her heart thump. Were they done already? She jumped to her feet, but it wasn't Abel and Lizzie outside. She frowned as she unlocked the door, not in the mood to deal with a stranger.

'Is she here?' the woman on the steps said without preamble or introduction.

'I'm sorry?' Genie said, folding her arms across her chest, her hackles up. She'd never seen this woman before, but she'd know those eyes anywhere.

'Don't give me that,' the woman said, rolling her eyes. 'Get her out here right now. She's skipping school.'

Genie hadn't given a thought to the fact that Lizzie was still of school age. 'She isn't here.'

'You're lying. Whoever you are.' The woman – their mother, Genie supposed, though it didn't feel right even thinking of her that way - tried to look past Genie into the theatre. 'Elizabeth!'

she called out in a harsh voice. 'Get your backside out here this minute!'

'I've told you once. She isn't here,' Genie sighed. She wanted rid of this woman and fast and gambled on the best way to do it. 'Check for yourself if you like.'

Abel and Lizzie's mother looked at Genie suspiciously and then stepped past her into the foyer. She was shorter by a head, a slight figure in a fake leather skirt. Genie watched as she stuck her head into the auditorium and then came back out and stood in the centre of the foyer.

'This place needs bulldozing,' she observed, curling her lip.

Genie ignored her, still standing by the door. 'Have you seen enough?'

The other woman narrowed her eyes, her face calculating. 'She's been here today, hasn't she?'

'No,' Genie said, glad that she didn't need to lie.

'I'm surprised he's living in such a dump,' Abel's mother said, and the careless way she referred to her son made Genie's hand itch to grab her and fling her out. 'If he's still here, that is. He doesn't stick around. He lives a charmed life these days. God only knows how.'

'I think you should leave now,' Genie said, keeping her voice indifferent.

'I bet you do.' The smaller woman's brittle smile didn't touch her eyes. 'I know she's meeting him, so don't even bother lying for them.'

Genie didn't. She just stood there with the door held open, waiting for her unwelcome visitor to give up and leave. She didn't.

'Maybe I'll just wait around here for them.' There was a sort of veiled threat in the words, making Genie dislike her all the more. The woman shoved her hand into her coat pocket and pulled out a box of cigarettes. 'Smoke?'

'No. You can't do that here, it's no smoking,' Genie said firmly, all the same aware that citing their smoking policy seemed rather a moot point given the state of the place. Abel's mother laughed and lit a cigarette anyway, a none too subtle challenge to Genie's authority. It was difficult to see how a woman with so few discernible redeeming qualities had managed to produce two decent human beings as offspring.

Behind her Genie heard voices, and turning, she saw Abel and Lizzie coming up the steps, laughing together. For a split second her heart leapt at the simple sight of his beautiful smile; and then panic set in right after.

'Abel, Lizzie,' she said, shaking her head and trying to alert them to oncoming trouble with her eyes.

Too late. The smiles slid abruptly from their faces as their mother stepped into the doorway behind Genie.

'What the fuck is she doing here?' he said, looking from Genie to his mother and back again.

Beside him, Lizzie gasped then turned to make a run for it. Abel shot his mother a murderous look and then cursed and followed his sister, catching up with her easily at the bottom of the steps.

'Lizzie, don't run,' he whispered, gathering her to him and speaking against the top of her head. 'It's the worst thing you can do. Trust me. It's taken me a lot of years to work that one out.' He set her away from him, his hands on her fragile shoulders as he looked down into her big, tearful eyes. He could feel her palpable anxiety, and he understood just how much she wanted to run and keep on running. 'You're not on your own now Lizzie, okay? Come on. We'll do it together.'

She nodded, and let him lead her back up the steps with his arm around her shoulders.

'How did you know where to find me?' Lizzie asked, staring baldly at her mother.

'Because I know you, Elizabeth. As soon as the school called to say you weren't there again I knew I'd find you sneaking around this place. I knew you wouldn't keep your nose out, despite what I said.' She dropped her cigarette onto the stone steps and ground it out with her shoe. 'You're a stupid, disobedient girl and you'll come to a bad end. Come on. We're leaving.'

Abel felt Lizzie stiffen beside him and held her closer against his side. 'She isn't coming with you.'

His mother's laughter was like nails down a blackboard. 'What's this, Abel? Big brother to the rescue?' She looked at Lizzie. 'He hasn't cared about you for the last fourteen years, Elizabeth. What do you think he's going to do?' Lizzie stiffened, and Abel hated his mother more than ever in that moment. 'I'll tell you, shall I?' his mother went on. 'He'll give you five minutes of his precious time and then disappear again.'

'That's not exactly what happened, is it?' he said. 'You never saw fit to even tell me I had a sister.'

'Half sister,' his mother corrected, ever spiteful.

'She's my fucking sister,' Abel said, stepping up so close to his mother that she stepped backwards inside the theatre.

He followed her in, Lizzie's small hand in his. He was aware of Genie on the edges of this circus and hated that she had to witness it.

Their mother looked them both over assessingly then lit up a fresh cigarette and blew the smoke slowly into the air.

'Do you want to know why I never told you about her?' she said, her tone conversational.

Pin drop silence echoed around the foyer. He watched her, hating that her explanation even mattered to him.

'Because you knew I'd take her from you?' he retorted, aware of the sound of Lizzie's soft gasp beside him.

Lazy amusement crossed his mother's face, as if she found the notion absurd.

'I did it to protect her from you, Abel.' The revelation winded him like a punch in the guts. 'I knew you'd turn on her like you turned on me. Because that's what you do, son. You abandon people.'

He opened his mouth but the words wouldn't come. She was

wrong, the rational part of his adult brain knew it, but the emotional side of it pressed forward, greedy to agree with his mother. He had abandoned her. But worse than that, he'd let history repeat itself; he'd turned on then abandoned Genie. Would he abandon Lizzie in time too? Was he a terrible, unreliable man?

He could see the triumph slide into his mother's eyes. She'd got him and she knew it.

Except she hadn't counted on Genie.

Wow, their mother was a piece of work. Genie had forced herself to stand by and watch as she worked her children like puppets, but she couldn't let it go on any longer. Abel's faltering uncertainty filled her with rage on his behalf, and she found herself stepping forward to stand between them.

'Enough,' she said, staring his mother down, her voice low and deadly serious. 'This ends here. You don't get to come here and spout your crap in my theatre. You don't get to come here and pass judgement on a man you neither know nor love. Do you hear me?'

His mother stared at her appraisingly, her hands on her hips. 'You'll see. He'll leave you soon enough,' she said, taking a long, slow drag on her cigarette.

Genie saw red and stepped forward, plucking the cigarette right out from the other woman's fingers and dropping it to the floor. She stamped on it and then looked back up, blazing.

'I never knew my mother,' Genie told her, shaking inside with red hot fury. 'And right now I'm just glad she had the decency to leave me with someone who'd love me rather than do her best to screw me up. And you know what? You've failed. Spectacularly. Getting away from you was the single best thing Abel ever did, because in spite of you he's managed to grow up into the best man I've ever known.'

All of the pent up emotion she'd held deep inside spilled out right there and then for them all to see.

'You failed because he's good, and he's kind, and he's decent,' she said, her voice ringing clear and strong around the foyer. 'You failed because he's funny, and he's honest, and he's loyal.' She moved closer. 'But most of all, you failed because despite your best efforts, he's happy, and he knows how to make other people happy.' Genie turned at the touch of his hand on her shoulder. The look in his eyes told her all she needed to know. 'He makes me happy, and he'll make Lizzie happier than she's ever been,' she said, feeling the younger girl move to stand at her other side.

They stood there united, Genie in the centre, Abel's arm around her shoulders, Lizzie's hand clutching onto hers.

'You can leave now,' Genie said, her blazing eyes daring their mother to defy her.

For a moment it looked as if she might, as if she were scrabbling around for something clever to say. In the end she said nothing, just shook her head and stalked out as if it had been her idea to leave in the first place.

Beside her, Genie felt Lizzie begin to cry, and she turned and wrapped her arms around the younger girl.

'Sshhh, it's okay,' she murmured, holding her tight. Abel wrapped his arms around the both of them, kissing the top of Genie's head, resting his chin on her, comforting her every bit as much as she comforted Lizzie.

'You lied,' Lizzie said, taking a seat with Genie in the cafe again a little while later. 'He *is* your boyfriend, isn't he?'

Genie's eyes followed Abel as he chatted easily with the guy behind the counter.

'No. He isn't, but I wish he was,' she murmured, as much to herself as to Lizzie. How very much she wished he was hers.

Lizzie rolled her eyes in that way that teenagers do, as if they think adults are the dumbest people on the planet. She'd cried herself dry back in the theatre and seemed to feel much better for it.

'Ask him then. I'm pretty sure he'd say yes.'

Genie smiled sadly. 'It's not as simple as that.' She shrugged, struggling to summarise what had happened between them in a way that was suitable for teenage ears. 'Stuff happened with us... it's kind of complicated.'

She looked up as Abel made his way across to their table with three mugs.

'Hot chocolate,' he said, sliding a mug topped with whipped cream and chocolate sprinkles towards Lizzie. She grinned, scooping up cream with her finger and licking it with her eyes closed blissfully. Abel placed a cappuccino in front of Genie then pulled up a chair and sat down.

'So, Lizzie. You're never going home again,' he said, right off the bat. Lizzie's eyes opened wide. 'Unless you want to, that is,' Abel added, as an afterthought.

Lizzie shook her head. 'Oh my God, no! But where will I go?' She squared her shoulders, suddenly frowning. 'Will I have to go back into care again?' she asked, still far more a child than a woman.

'No way,' Abel said, straight to the point. 'Come and live with me.'

Lizzie gawked. 'In Australia?'

Abel nodded. 'You'll like it. The sun shines, and I live on the beach.'

Laughter bubbled up from Lizzie's chest as she clamped her hands flat against her cheeks. 'Can I really?'

Genie smiled when Lizzie's shining, excited eyes moved between them both. She looked younger than ever without the heavy make-up that her crying session had washed away, and already well on the way with that big brother hero worship thing. Genie loved him for the simple way he took Lizzie's fears and squashed them beneath his boots, and envied the younger girl so much that she could barely speak.

'I'll be back in a sec,' she said, scraping her chair back and heading quickly for the safety of the bathroom to take some deep breaths and pull herself together.

Abel watched Genie walk away with his brows knitted together.

'Is she your girlfriend?' Lizzie asked, stirring the cream into her hot chocolate with a long spoon. 'Because I like her a lot.'

Abel dragged his eyes back to his sister. 'No. I like her a lot too though.'

'I don't get it. You like her. She likes you. What's the problem?'

He didn't know how to answer that. There were lots of problems.

'Just drink your chocolate,' he said, softening his words with a small smile.

Lizzie sipped her drink and then set her mug back down, still eyeing him speculatively. 'She's pretty though, isn't she?'

Abel sighed. Pretty didn't begin to cover it. She was his kind of beautiful, he knew that now. 'I guess,' he said, cursing himself for sounding even more juvenile than his kid sister.

Genie re-emerged from the bathroom and he watched her pick her way lightly back towards their table, arching her back to squeeze between two chairs, reminding him of how she'd arched beneath him over the lamp. His body kicked in, appreciating the memory more than he'd like to admit. She'd surprised him back there at the theatre today. More than that. She'd awed him, and she'd humbled him with her protective strength, turning herself into a goddamn warrior princess right in front of his eyes.

He'd come to London all those months ago expecting to teach it a lesson, and instead he'd been given a master class in life skills by Genie Divine. She'd had her own unconventional upbringing, and she'd taken it on the chin, run with it, and turned it into a life full of glittering positives. She'd never known either of her parents, and yet she remained the most secure person he knew, forging her own path through life, unencumbered by the crippling need to compensate for the shortfalls of others.

If she could do it, then maybe he could too, and maybe in

time he could teach Lizzie the same attitude. Jesus, he hoped so. Reaching for his coffee he knocked back a bitter mouthful and looked away as Genie sat back down.

Lizzie hugged Genie tightly outside the cafe a little while later. 'Will I see you soon?' she said, her dark eyes hopeful when she stepped back.

Genie looked quickly at Abel and then back to Lizzie. 'I'm sure you will,' she said brightly, putting her bag over her shoulder. 'And you can always call me.'

Lizzie felt around in her pockets for her phone. 'I don't have your number…'

'I have it,' Abel said quickly, not quite meeting Genie's eyes. She didn't let herself remember how sizzlingly sexy it had been, writing her number onto his bare skin. It seemed a lifetime ago now. Would she still have let things play out between them as they had, if she'd known? There wasn't really any question. It was hard to regret loving someone when they'd made you feel everything more brightly and deeply and fully than ever before. The stars were more dazzling, desserts tasted sweeter; life was just bigger and better in every way for having him around. She knew this with certainty, now that he was here, however fleetingly, once again. Things may not have turned out how she wished they would, but she'd never regret him, or forget him.

The tricky bit was learning how to live on the opposite side of the world from him without crawling into bed and staying there forever.

'Genie,' he dipped his head now to brush his lips over her cheek in goodbye. 'I'll call you,' he murmured, tucking her hair behind her ear. She looked down at the pavement, choked up, nodding.

'Okay.'

She watched him walk away, and grew lonelier with every step he took.

Abel noticed the bookshop just around the corner and steered Lizzie inside.

'What are we doing?' she said, twisting to look up at him.

'Buying you books.' She'd mentioned earlier that she loved to read. He was already looking out for any opportunity to do kind things for her, to give her some of the generosity and thoughtfulness that he knew full well had been missing from her so-called home life up to now. 'A girl who loves to read needs books,' he told her. He pushed her forward gently. 'Go choose some. As many as you like.'

He stepped outside, leaving Lizzie happily browsing the new releases. Pulling his phone from inside his jacket, he tapped out the words he hadn't been able to say.

'You were amazing today. Dinner tonight?'

She didn't make him wait. His phone buzzed within a minute.

Around the corner, Genie sagged against the wall with relief.

'Yes,' she typed, pressing send.

'God, yes,' she whispered, tipping her head back and watching the clouds scuttle across the sky. 'Yes.'

Chapter Nineteen

Genie climbed out of her cab in front of the same hotel where she'd met Abel way back when. If possible, she was even more nervous this time around than last time. She hadn't known him then, and she'd had an agenda.

Her only agenda tonight was to speak from her heart and hope that he'd listen.

She was early, mostly because she was running on anxious energy and couldn't bear to sit around. She'd dressed carefully and then changed twice, settling in the end for a long-sleeved black wrap dress and heels. It had been a close call versus turning up in jeans and tee shirt. She wasn't interested in dinner or small talk or candles. She just needed to hear his truths, to know whether she needed to try and work out how to live without him.

Would he be in the bar, like last time? Probably not, if Lizzie was with him. She walked across the marble floored reception and put her head inside the bar to check. A second later, the hairs on the back of her neck stood up. He was behind her, his hand on her elbow.

'Genie,' he said, and she turned to him, swallowing hard. He was alone.

'Where's Lizzie?'

'Upstairs. She's in the room next to mine with pizza, movies and a pile of new books. She looked all in, poor kid.'

'It's been quite a day for her,' Genie said. 'For both of you.'

He looked at her steadily. 'For all of us.' His fingers massaged her elbow. 'I thought we'd eat upstairs. Unless you'd rather…' he glanced around then stopped speaking when she shook her head.

'Upstairs,' she said, quickly. The kind of intensely personal conversation they needed to have wasn't for crowded restaurants or strangers' ears.

Abel's hand lay warm against the base of her spine as he led her to the elevator and stepped inside, leaning his back against the mirrors. Genie stood alongside him, her eyes on the ceiling as they both tried and failed not to remember the last time they'd been here. She could hear his breathing, slightly too fast, and only let her own breath out in a whoosh when the doors opened for them to step outside into the carpeted corridor.

Pausing for a second outside Lizzie's door, Abel leaned his ear towards it. 'All quiet,' he said, and then moved and opened the door to the next room along. Swinging it wide, he stepped aside for her to come inside with him.

'Are you hungry?' he said, throwing the key card into the pool of light on the lamp table.

Genie shook her head. 'Not a bit.'

He pulled a bottle of wine from the mini bar and poured a couple of glasses as she perched on the sofa. Taking a glass from his outstretched fingers as he drew near, she sipped from it gratefully, Abel sitting down beside her, not quite touching, but close.

How could it feel so weird and formal? They'd seen each other at their most exposed, yet they were as awkward as strangers. The air around them was heavy, loaded and tense, as if the whole place might go up if someone lit a match.

'I lied to you, Genie,' he said softly, breaking the silence.

She turned to look at him, braced for him to go on, not sure if they were on the verge of goodbye or the verge of forever.

'In the lift at the hospital, when I told you it was just fucking. I lied.'

Tiny little birds of hope fluttered behind her rib cage. 'You had your reasons.' Was she excusing him, or asking a question?

'Oh, I thought I did,' he said. 'I thought I knew you, but I didn't. I didn't know you at all. I was so hell bent on separating you from your job in my head that I didn't let myself see the whole, real, beautiful woman standing right in front of me all along.'

He slid his glass onto the table. 'I see you now. I see you just as you are.' Taking her glass from her, he placed it next to his on the table then threaded his fingers through hers. 'I watched you handle my mother this afternoon, so brave and full of conviction, and I couldn't believe I'd been such a fool not coming back for you sooner. Every day back home I've fought the urge to catch the next plane. Your email… I came because of Lizzie, but I was always coming back for you anyway. I just needed to find a way to climb over my own stupid pride first. '

Genie stroked his fingers, studying them as he spoke, his words a balm over the lacerations that criss-crossed her heart. 'It was never you that needed to change, Beauty,' he said, choked up. 'It was always me.'

Genie turned to face him, and the expression in his eyes brought tears to hers too.

'You don't need to say these things,' she said, laying her hand against the warmth of his face, tracing over his cheekbone with her thumb. 'I've regretted that night a hundred times over, Abel. I pushed you, and I pushed you, and I had no clue how much I was hurting you. When I think of how you looked just before the ceiling came down…' she shuddered, hating the memory. 'I'm so, so sorry.'

He turned his lips into her palm and kissed it, resting his forehead against hers with his eyes closed.

'Don't,' he said. 'Don't say you're sorry. I don't want you to be.' He moved slightly, stroking his hand over her hair. 'I took what I wanted from you over and over again and then made you feel bad for it. I was just so fucking greedy for you that I couldn't think straight.'

He kissed her at last, a slow, trembling brush of mouth on

mouth, the raw tangle of emotion and relief and lust as powerful as a punch in the solar plexus. Genie melted into him, loving his arms as they moved around her to hold her close, loving his mouth as his tongue slid slowly across hers, loving his strength and his humility and his heart.

'I should have told you that I loved you in that elevator,' he went on, lifting his head to look at her. 'I knew it, but I didn't say it. I walked away from you, just like she said I would.'

Genie held his face between her hands. 'Don't ever say that again,' she said, urgently. 'Your mother was trying to make you feel bad to cover up her own shortcomings. I won't let you take those insults on your shoulders, Abel, you hear me?'

He heard her, and he believed her, because he loved the way she lived her life with clarity and optimism. His defences were on the floor, and his need to hold her was sky high. He didn't care if he got the showgirl or the backstage sweetheart anymore. He finally understood that they were two halves of the same glorious girl, and he needed her curves and her laughter and her sanity to make sense of his fucked up world.

'Come to bed with me,' he said, his voice rough with the need for her to say yes.

Genie took both of his hands in hers and brought his knuckles to her mouth, grazing her lips across them with her eyes closed. Her tears washed between his fingers, and he flexed his hands and held her face up to his.

'Don't cry any more, Beauty,' he said, thumbing away her tears, drawing her onto his lap to lift her into his arms. Any other time she might have protested, ever the independent woman. Not this time. She let him carry her to his bed, and when he laid her down she pulled him down with her.

'Don't let me go,' she breathed, her fingers working the buttons of his shirt free and pushing it away from his body. She was delicate beneath him, glass-like; he knew he could break her all too easily. He'd tried to break her spirit, and he'd nigh on broken her heart, and yet here she was, giving herself to him all over again.

She had the biggest heart of anyone he'd ever met and, crazily, she wanted to give it to him. They'd fucked, and they'd fought, but they'd never made love like this. He'd never made love with anyone like this.

Opening her dress, he lifted her out of it, leaving her lying on his sheets in scant black lace. Knowing that they had all night and that neither of them was playing to win any more stripped away the previous urgency of their sex, exposing the tenderness and yearning that lay beneath.

Unclipping her bra, he swept the lace aside and held both of her hands in one of his own loosely over her head. He'd seen her breasts before. He knew what to expect, so why did he feel as if he were looking at her for the very first time? The lushness of her curves sent the blood rushing to his brain, blotting out every last thought that wasn't about the girl beneath him.

'I love the way you look at me,' she whispered, and he lowered his head to kiss her, taking the warmth of her breath into his mouth as she sighed with pleasure. He slid his hand down the column of her neck as her tongue moved with his, her back curving into a graceful arch when his fingers covered the soft roundness of her breasts.

'You're so incredibly lovely, Genie,' he said, letting his usually guarded thoughts tumble out against her lips. 'So fucking incredibly lovely.'

He felt her body respond to his words, felt her emotions deepen their kiss into something close to sacred. Her hands slipped from his and went around his shoulders, stroking his back, holding him to her.

'I want you, Abel,' she said softly. 'I've ached for you, here.' She moved his hand over her heart, and then down her body, between her legs. 'I ache all the time. I think about you, and I want you, and I ache.'

He nodded, kissing her eyes when she closed them. He knew, because he ached too.

'You don't need to ache anymore,' he said gently, kissing the curve of her neck as he moved her underwear down her hips. Genie raised her body to help him and then opened her legs.

'Tell me what you need,' he said, resting his hand over the heat of her. 'This,' as he moved his fingers between her lips and found her wet for him, and the urge to take the decision from her almost overwhelmed him. 'Or this…' Abel flicked his tongue over Genie's mouth, knowing how goddamn good she'd taste if he slid down between her legs. 'Or this, Genie?' he said, and rocked his hips into hers, nestling his cock between her thighs until they both moaned.

There wasn't really any question to answer.

Genie reached between them and unbuttoned his jeans, and Abel kicked them off and settled back between her thighs, flaring her knee out with his flattened palm.

Stroking her hair from her face, his fingers knotted with hers beside her head on the pillows. Beautiful, beautiful girl. Damp auburn tendrils clung to her flushed cheeks, and the tiniest of breathless, agonised smiles touched her lips.

'Ready?' he said, knowing full well that she was from the way her body undulated against his. She nodded, her eyes half closed and her mouth kiss-swollen as he slid his cock slowly against her clitoris, building her higher. He wanted to remember her forever like this, open and wanting him so badly that she trembled beneath him. So deeply, erotically sexy that he couldn't wait any more. Positioning himself against her, he pushed, sinking all the way inside her body, making her gasp.

Genie tangled herself around him, no spaces, no air, and even if he lived to be a hundred Abel knew he'd never feel such a rush of perfect, intense completeness. For a few seconds it was all he could to hold still and keep breathing.

And then he started to move, a slow, deep grind, loving the way her body held him inside.

'Look at me,' he said against her ear, and when he lifted his head, the look in her eyes set him on fire. She was so close to coming, breathless and boneless with it, drenched and hot in his hands and around his cock. He thrust harder for her, and then for himself, because when she hit the top she unexpectedly took his control right along with her own.

Burying his face in her neck, Abel let go, spilling himself inside her as she shook and clung to him, and him to her.

'It isn't just fucking,' he whispered.

What had happened between them in that bed was a long way beyond sex, beyond fucking, beyond making love, even. It was a union of bodies and hearts and lives and love, the kind of big, once in a lifetime love that leaves you with no choice but to surrender to it and be together.

Wrapped around each other later, Genie listened to Abel's steady heartbeat beneath her ear as he kissed the top of her head.

'I bought your theatre for you,' he said, low key.

She pushed herself up on her elbows and stared at him. He smoothed her hair out of her eyes gently, waiting for her to gather herself together and say something.

'For me?'

'Yes. For you. Not for a gym. To make it a real theatre again. It's yours by right.'

'I don't know what to say,' she said after a long, disbelieving pause, blown away. 'Thank you doesn't seem enough.'

Abel hadn't just bought her her home back. He'd given her her life back, if she wanted it, and in doing so he'd said 'I love you for everything you are,' which was all she'd ever wanted to hear him say.

'There's just one problem,' he said, twisting strands of her hair around his fingers. 'I want you to come and live in Australia with me.'

Genie had been so envious of Lizzie when Abel had made her the same offer earlier that day. Knowing that his plans included her too made her feel extraordinary, cherished, truly loved.

'Or I'll come here to you,' he said, uncertain in the face of her wondering silence.

Genie treasured him all the more for making the offer because she knew how much it would cost him to leave his beloved adopted country. She'd spent so long desperately trying to hang onto the theatre and all she thought she held dear. For now, just knowing that her old life was there for her if she wanted it turned out to be enough. Maybe there was more than one way to be happy.

'I've never been to Australia,' she said, feeling quiet excitement well up inside her. 'Maybe you could show me.'

He pulled her against him. 'You'll love it. I promise you.'

Genie lay in the circle of his arms, tracing patterns on his chest with her fingertips.

'You kind of blew it with your prospective mother in law this afternoon,' he said, and she could hear the quiet laughter behind his words. She loved him for his light-heartedness, and even more for the proposal that lay casually hidden in his words.

'I love you very much,' she said, holding him close in her arms and her heart.

Abel kissed her forehead. 'You too, Beauty. You too.'

Genie listened to his breathing even out as they fell towards sleep, her head full of half formed thoughts about how theirs would be the best kind of family, dictated by choice and love rather than by blood and obligation.

Abel Kingdom. The smallest of smiles touched Genie's lips. If someone had told her a few months ago that he was to be her forever man, she'd have argued herself blind. She'd expected to find very little to like beneath his beautiful, masculine exterior, but she'd never been more wrong.

He was strong, and he was loyal. He was bold, and he was kind. The man was one hundred percent solid gold, and he was one hundred percent hers.

Epilogue ~ Ten years later, Sydney, Australia.

'London! You're so lucky, Lizzie,' Erin said. 'I'm so coming over to see you while you're there.'

'I'm counting on it,' Lizzie laughed, handing her best friend one of her own secret blend cocktails. 'Come and help me take these out by the pool?'

Erin tasted the clear red cocktail in the fine-stemmed martini glass and rolled her eyes. 'I'm going to miss you loads, Liz, but I'll miss your cocktails more. You have to tell me what's in this one as a parting gift!'

Lizzie winked. 'It's my latest.' She sipped it and then grinned. 'It's bloody good, isn't it? I call it The Divine Spirit.'

She'd been developing a range of signature cocktails for months and was looking forward to trying them out on the customers at the Divine Bar in London. Flutters of excitement filled her heart at the thought of her travel plans for the next six months. First stop London for a two month residency as guest bar manager at Theatre Divine, then onward to New York and finally Tokyo before coming home again to Australia in time for Christmas.

Circulating in the opposite direction to Erin with a tray of cocktails, she paused beside Genie and offered her a drink.

'Wow!' Genie said, her trademark mile-wide smile brighter than ever. 'These look stunning. Deanna's going to have to watch out in London, you'll have all the customers propping up the bar instead of watching the show!'

'That's kind of my plan.' Lizzie grinned back, her dark ponytail swinging as she moved away to hand out the drinks to the many friends who'd gathered to come and see her off on her big adventure.

Genie watched her walk out into the sunshine, her heart squeezing tight at the idea of Lizzie flying the nest. She was so proud of the confident, beautiful young woman Abel's sister had blossomed into over the last ten years. Australia really had been the making of her. Genie loved her as a sister, a daughter and a friend, and she was going to miss her enormously.

'Hey you.'

She closed her eyes and enjoyed the little thrill that always rippled down her spine at the touch of Abel's warm fingers on the back of her neck. Dropping a kiss onto the shoulder exposed by her wide necked tee shirt, he settled behind her against the kitchen work surface, his hand casually on her waist.

'Okay?' he asked, against her hair.

'Yeah,' she sighed, looking around the airy, open plan kitchen that led out onto the pool. 'I know it's the best thing for Lizzie, but I'm just going to miss her.'

Abel laughed softly. 'You've got enough chicks left here to cluck over, Beauty,' he said.

'I know, I know. But London…'

Abel turned her around to face him, a beer in one hand, his other playing idly with the ties at the neck of her bikini. Lizzie had insisted on a casual pool party for her send off, which suited them well as a bohemian family of beach bums. Abel still rocked faded jeans and a tee shirt better than any other man Genie knew; he seemed to just get better and better with age. Leaning into him, she breathed his familiar clean, beachy smell in deep.

'London won't know what's hit it when Lizzie gets there,' he said quietly, taking her fears seriously. 'And you know how much Davey's dying to see her.'

'I know, and I know Deanna's the perfect person to watch

out for her while she's there, it's just… oh I know.' She shrugged her shoulders. 'Ignore me, I'm being stupid.'

And in her heart of hearts, she knew that she was. There couldn't have been a more perfect time for Lizzie to head back to experience London life for herself.

The theatre was back to its best; better than ever if she was honest, under Deanna's creative directorship for the last decade. They'd worked together through ambitious plans in the early years to rebuild the place from the ground up, and once polished it had deservedly become the most lustrous jewel in the London burlesque crown.

The Divine Girls had fast gathered a reputation as one of the sexiest dance troupes in Europe, and review sites now ranked them alongside the top Parisian shows for both spectacle and glitz. Competition was fierce each year to secure a spot in the troupe: dancers came from all over the world to be amongst the few chosen to perform on the stage that had once been smashed and ruined by falling rafters. It was a fitting way to honour the place that had been Genie's home for so many years, and although she'd hung up her own performing heels, her love for the place still shone bright.

Abel pulled her closer. 'You're not being stupid. I don't much like the thought of her in London either if I'm honest, but look at her.' They watched Lizzie as she moved easily between her friends, long limbed and tanned in denim cut offs. 'She's not that frightened kid any more, and God knows she's not going back there with screwed up crazy ideas of righting any wrongs.'

He knocked back a good mouthful of chilled beer, and Genie wrapped her arm around his back to slide her hand inside his tee shirt and stroke the smooth warmth of his skin.

'She's lucky you were there,' she said softly, remembering the difficult times.

'She's luckier that you were,' Abel said, massaging her shoulder. 'I listen to her sometimes and I can hear you in her words.'

Genie looked up at him, moved. 'Really?'

He nodded. 'She's got that same attitude, that optimism. Thanks to you she walks around with her glass half full.'

Tears welled in Genie's throat; it meant such a lot to hear those words from Abel. Even though his mother had died four short years after they left London, her children would always carry the scars of their childhoods with them. Genie loved them both fiercely, and over time her love had turned out to be the band-aid the Kingdom children had needed to pick themselves up, dust themselves down, and little by little, let themselves be happy.

'Dad!'

Genie and Abel both turned as their six-year-old son came skidding into the room, a trail of his friends behind him.

'Is it time for the cake yet? We're starving!'

'When are you not starving, Rubes?' Abel said, ruffling Reuben's dark hair affectionately. 'You better ask your mum. She's the cake queen around here.'

'Not long,' Genie promised. She'd baked a huge version of Lizzie's favourite chocolate cake, a recipe they'd honed together over the years. Genie had never baked so much as a jam tart before moving to Australia; it had just seemed like something she and Lizzie might be able to learn together. They'd become something of a crack team in the kitchen, and Lizzie had taken her passion for food and drink and turned it into what promised to be an exciting career.

'Go get all the kids together by the pool and I'll bring it out,' she said, shooing the children out towards the autumn sunshine.

'I'll go get the twins,' Abel said, dropping a kiss on Genie's forehead before heading out of the kitchen to the nursery upstairs.

Glancing at the clock, she reckoned that he'd find the babies wide awake by now. They'd been asleep for over an hour already, and at just turned two years old they were at the age where they viewed daytime naps as an unwelcome interruption to mayhem.

Genie watched him leave and stood alone for a moment, absently turning her wedding ring around on her finger as she looked fondly around the big, comfortable kitchen. They'd spent the last ten years building their family here.

Abel. Genie. Lizzie. Reuben. Amber. Jamie.

Letting one of them head out into the world alone for an adventure was going to be hard on her heart, but she knew that wherever Lizzie went, she travelled safe in the knowledge that her home and her family were right here waiting for her to come home again.

Much later that evening, when the party had dwindled and a legion of stars pricked the night sky, Abel sat in one of the deep sofas out on the deck and watched the ocean.

'Penny for them?' Genie said softly, joining him outside with a couple of glasses of brandy in her hands.

He looked at her, her long hair tied up messily after an afternoon in and out of the pool, sun-kissed and beautiful in the black sundress she'd thrown over her bikini, and he wasn't even sure how to put his thoughts into words.

'I'm proud of you,' he said. 'Proud of everything you've achieved since you came here.'

Genie settled onto the other end of the sofa and tucked her feet underneath him. She looked surprised by his words as she sipped her brandy. She shouldn't be. Even though he'd tried his best to make it clear that he didn't mind if she wanted to carry on performing, she'd chosen instead to develop a burlesque-based exercise class, starting locally and then rolling it out quickly across all of his gyms when it caught on like wildfire. It had become a surprise sensation, and she'd revelled in her brand new business, growing her range of sexy exercise clothing and classes year on year. It was so very Genie to think of a way to allow as many other women as possible to feel empowered and beautiful while also allowing him to have her all to himself. He hadn't asked it of her, yet she'd chosen to give it to him anyway.

Leaning forwards, she kissed him lingeringly and then lay back with her head in his lap.

'I'm proud of you too,' she said, closing her eyes as he unpicked the band from her hair and combed it through with his fingers. Mellow music floated on the air from the remnants of the party at the back of the house, and slowly, slowly, Abel's massage turned from relaxing to sensual. Her head, and then her shoulders, and then a slow stroke over the hollow at the base of her neck. It was always this way with them; he had a special way of touching her, and it had only grown more spine-tinglingly intimate with the passing years.

When his fingers moved down to cup her breast through the thin material of her dress, she pulled his hand to her mouth and kissed his palm, the band of his wedding ring cool against her cheek.

'Come on,' she said. 'Let's go to bed.'

He glanced down at his swollen jeans, and then ruefully towards the lingering party-goers he needed to walk though. 'I better wait five before I follow you up.'

Genie laughed softly, kissing him as she got to her feet.

'Teenager,' she whispered, winding her way back into the lit up beach house.

Abel picked up his brandy and sighed with bone deep contentment, his eyes on the dark horizon, his mind on Genie. He could still see her as she'd been the first time he'd ever laid eyes on her, dancing on that theatre stage back in London. She'd dazzled him then, and she'd gone on to dazzle him even more every day since.

It was no good. Thinking of her peeling her clothes off on stage was doing nothing to calm him down. Knocking back the last of his brandy, he headed inside in search of his wife.

THE END

ABOUT THE AUTHOR

USA Today best selling author Kitty French lives in the
UK with her husband and their two little boys.

Kitty also writes steamy romantic comedy under the
pseudonym Kat French. Undertaking Love is out now
from HarperCollins.

SIGN UP FOR KITTY'S NEWSLETTER!
If you'd like to receive news and snippets about Kitty's
upcoming books, please email on
kittyfrenchwriter@me.com to sign up for her newsletter.

GET IN TOUCH WITH KITTY
Twitter: @kittysbooks
Facebook: Kitty French
Email: kittyfrenchwriter@me.com
Website: www.kittyfrench.com

A NOTE FROM THE AUTHOR

Thanks so much for reading Genie. I really hope you enjoyed it, and would love it if you have a second to post a review to help guide other readers.

I've got a top-secret project coming up next, more news very soon on my Facebook page and newsletter.

Until next time,

Kitty x

ACKNOWLEDGMENTS

As always I owe a debt of gratitude to my lovely friend and editor Charlie Hobson. I honestly wouldn't want to write these books without you, you push me to think deeper and work harder and my books are so much better for it. You're all-round fabulous!

Thanks also to Sarah Hansen at Okay Creations for the gorgeous cover, it's absolutely right for Genie and Abel's story.

A huge hi-five to all of the fabulous bloggers who always work so incredibly hard - thank you for your love of books, and for your unstinting support and encouragement. It means so much, I really am incredibly grateful.

Ditto my amazing Facebook and twitter buddies. As most of you know I've not had the best of years with my health, and you've all been so kind and patient and brilliant. It seemed at times as if this book would never actually come out, didn't it? Thank you for being there every day to talk about the small stuff that keeps my world turning.

Big love to the Minxes of Romance. I mean BIG. You guys are my writing family. Special love to Sally Clements for being a formatting whizzo.

Thanks also to my Bob bezzies for always being interested and cheering me on.

And last but never least, thank you to my own beloved people, my family. x

Made in the USA
Charleston, SC
09 March 2015